NORTH *by* NIGHT

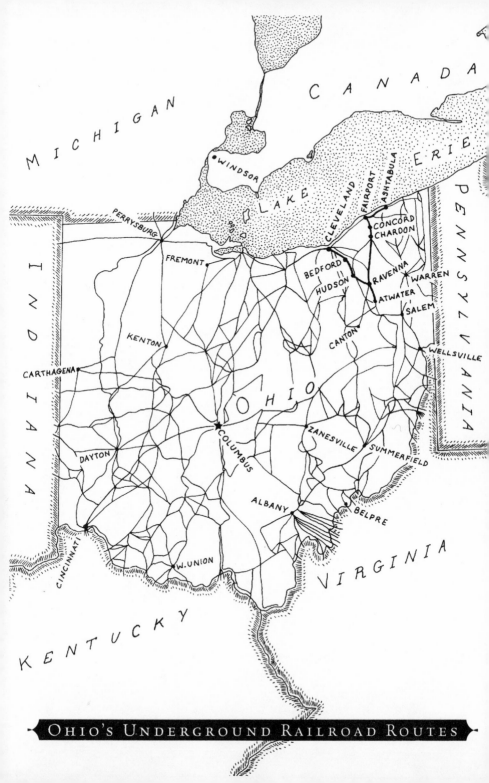

OHIO'S UNDERGROUND RAILROAD ROUTES

NORTH

by

NIGHT

A STORY OF THE
UNDERGROUND RAILROAD

Katherine Ayres

DELACORTE PRESS

Published by
DELACORTE PRESS
Bantam Doubleday Dell Publishing Group, Inc.
1540 Broadway
New York, New York 10036

Library of Congress Cataloging-in-Publication Data

Ayres, Katherine.
    North by night : a story of the underground railroad / Katherine
Ayres.
        p.   cm.
    Summary: Presents the journal of a sixteen-year-old girl whose
family operates a stop on the Underground Railroad.
    ISBN 0-385-32564-9
    1. Underground railroad—Juvenile fiction. [1. Underground
railroad—Fiction. 2. Fugitive slaves—Fiction. 3. Slavery—
Fiction. 4. Diaries—Fiction.]   I. Title.
PZ7.A9856No   1998   98-10039
                                                                          CIP
                                                                          AC

The text of this book is set in Centaur.
Book design by Semadar Megged
Manufactured in the United States of America
November 1998
10   9   8   7   6   5   4   3   2   1

For the piano man

*And to honor the brave souls who rode the
Railroad and those who helped them ride*

Dear Reader,

Have you ever wondered what it would be like to live in another time? If you could travel months and years into the past or the future, would you do it? I've often thought about particular moments in history. And while I haven't yet discovered a time machine to carry me back, I can enter into the lives and times of others by writing novels that take place in the past. Sometimes I get so involved in the characters' predicaments, I'm startled to see members of my own family returning home, wearing modern clothing and carrying pizza boxes.

For this novel I asked myself a question: If I had lived in the time of slavery, would I have accepted it or fought against it? I spent weeks and weeks reading about the 1850s—about politics, Ohio, how much things cost, and how people traveled and lived and ate and worked. To help me write Lucinda's letters and those of the young men who admire her, I read real letters of young courting couples.

Then I studied slavery—Northern and Southern viewpoints, original slave narratives, abolitionists' writings. I found a book with yellowing pages, written in 1856, about fugitive slaves who escaped to Canada. I read newspaper reward notices for runaway slaves. I saw the tombstone of a slave child brought to Oberlin, Ohio, who died there at age four. As I studied slavery and the Underground Railroad I began to understand when, exactly, this story should take place.

In the fall of 1850 Congress passed the Fugitive Slave Act. This law required that runaway slaves be returned to their owners, even if they were captured on free Northern soil. Slave owners came north seeking runaways, or they hired catchers to track the fugitives down for them. After 1850 slaves had to make their way to Canada to find true freedom. In addition, the law required severe penalties for those who helped slaves to run—a fine of $1,000 and jail if convicted. In those days, an entire family farm—all the land, animals, and buildings—was worth about $1,000. One rescue put a whole family in danger.

If you want to write interesting books, you must put your characters in risky situations. To write about a girl working the Underground Railroad, I had to pick a time when the hazards were great. I set the book in the winter of 1851, just after the Fugitive Slave Act was passed, and then, to increase the risks even more, I included several runaways in the rescue.

I chose to set the book in Ohio partly because I was born there and it's familiar. But more important, Ohio in the 1850s seethed with conflict about slavery. Settlements of free blacks, Quakers, and fervent Presbyterians led the abolition movement and worked on the Underground Railroad. Again and again, they clashed with Southern sympathizers—neighbors who believed slaveholding was up to the individual, not the government.

I chose Ohio for geographical reasons, too. In 1850

Ohio provided the shortest passage from slave states to Canada, about 250 miles from the Ohio River to the Great Lakes. Slaves from Kentucky or Virginia (including what is now West Virginia) could travel over moderate terrain in Ohio, instead of across the rugged Allegheny Mountains in Pennsylvania. And travel they did—estimates range as high as thirty thousand passengers on Ohio's Underground Railroad routes.

Finally, as I did my research, I wanted to get not just the facts but the mood and social history right. I didn't want my contemporary thoughts to color the story and make it less believable.

Here's what I discovered: 1850 was a time of tremendous change. Industrial production and technological invention increased as subsistence farming diminished. People traveled more and on better roads, canals, and railroads. Families who had lived and worked on the same farm for generations suddenly found their sons and daughters moving to cities to take jobs in factories. Even those who didn't leave home caught the spirit of independence that blew across the land.

Therefore, it makes historical sense that Lucinda and her brother Will have an itch to travel, to go adventuring. The notion of a different life was suddenly possible, particularly on the frontier, where people valued feisty independence and where rigid traditions of proper behavior were relaxed.

As I read about the early women's rights movement, Miss Aurelia's character took shape. Women who believed in the abolition of slavery soon began to question sexual inequality. A husband owned and controlled all of his wife's property, and women could not vote or participate in political life. Women who expressed strong opinions and argued for the rights of others soon learned to use those skills in their own behalf.

These are the times and the places in which my fictional heroine Lucinda Spencer grew up. Her era was lively, changing, charged with political and social discontent. Imagine living then. Now step into my time machine. . . .

KATHERINE AYRES
Pittsburgh, 1997

NORTH *by* NIGHT

THOU SHALT NOT DELIVER UNTO HIS MASTER THE
SERVANT WHICH IS ESCAPED FROM HIS MASTER
UNTO THEE.

DEUTERONOMY 23:15

JANUARY

WEDNESDAY, JANUARY 1, 1851

ere begins the seventh journal in the life of myself, Lucinda Spencer, age sixteen, of the village of Atwater in the free state of Ohio.

Bless Papa and Mama for giving me a new writing book at Christmas. Last year's was nearly filled, and I had to squeeze in the news of our holiday celebrations and all the gifts. But I find it lovely to start a new journal on the first day of the new year.

The good Lord knows we ended last year badly and

need fresh hope for the future. Friend Eli Whitman of Salem was caught just three days past with a runaway slave wanted in Virginia. Caught! The word still sends shivers up my spine.

There is a harsh magistrate who lives in Canton, and a kinder one in Warren, so we are all praying that Friend Whitman will be judged in Warren, which lies much closer to Salem.

But do the magistrates give a peach pit for geography? Or for people's lives? Probably not. I'd like to fill the ears of these politicians—from members of the lowliest town council to the governor in Columbus and on to President Fillmore in his big house in Washington—with the stories I've heard.

Drat the president, anyway. Papa voted for him. President Fillmore is a Northern man, a New Yorker. So how could he let us down? How could he have signed that terrible law and brought such hardship on God's people?

Wild Canada geese, we call the runaways. Birds heading north, always north. We talk of flight paths, of migrations. Even now, as I sit here safe and warm, I know that somewhere there are birds with torn and tattered feathers, birds who travel cold, with empty stomachs and tired wings. Birds in hidden nests, and birds, even now, in flight.

Miranda is pulling on my arm and begging to write her name in my journal. She is at least as stubborn as I am, if not more. So I'd better let her write now and get it over with before she learns to spell out any more words— before she can read the thoughts I want to keep secret. I shall dip the pen carefully and guide her hand as she draws her letters so she doesn't make a blot on my first page. That would be a poor omen indeed to begin the year 1851.

Miranda

Gray and cloudy. I don't care for it one bit. A new year should be bright and shiny, like a new penny.

Thomas found a young injured doe in the woods this morning and brought her home. From the looks of her right hind leg, she got too close to a set of sharp teeth. He and Miranda are tending the frail thing in the barn.

William took one look at the deer, grinned, and said, "Venison."

Tom and Miranda outvoted him. Mama and Papa agreed.

I suggested we name her Titania, for the queen of the fairies. Tom likes Victoria, for the English queen. Miranda will think about the names and choose one, as she usually does. In either case, she'll raid Mama's yarn basket for colorful scraps and beg me to help her braid a queen's collar and crown for this newest waif.

The queen, whether Titania or Victoria, will join the others in the spare stall. Just now Tom and Miranda have

Hamlet, a duck who thinks he's a horse, Ophelia, a lop-sided chicken, and Brutus, a half-grown runty barn cat with a torn ear.

Will says Mama and Papa are soft with the younger two, but I disagree. I think our parents let them keep these creatures as pets since we can't have dogs, like most farm families do. Why, we can't even let any of the barn cats grow tame and come inside. For cats or dogs might make noise and give everything away. All the strays have to stay in the barn, at a safe distance. I help with this by pretending to sneeze whenever I get too close to fur.

But still, someday when we no longer need to keep such a quiet house, wouldn't it be nice to have a puppy?

Friday, January 3, 1851

Gray, gray, and more gray. Sometimes I think winter wears a drab Quaker's dress. But I am a Presbyterian! I am allowed bright colors. Will the sun ever return?

Saturday, January 4, 1851

Tonight is more than half gone, yet I sit here and shiver beside the fire, unable to sleep. Pictures run through my mind; I hear echoes of Friend Whitman's capture. He will be bound over for a hearing with the harsh man in Canton. Worse luck.

My night's adventure started as it usually does, with a sound—pebbles at the window brought me awake. My heartbeat quickened and energy surged through me like flames. I reached under the bed for my boots and for

William's outgrown corduroy trousers and thick woolen jacket.

The bare floor chilled my feet as I crept from the bed, taking care not to awaken Miranda. I stole from our room, my odd clothing bundled under one arm, and made my way to the dark kitchen.

Like an owl in the night, I listened for the smallest rustle while I drew on the trousers, then the boots. As I buttoned the old woolen jacket over my nightgown the knocks came. Two short raps. Silence. Then two more.

I strode to the door. "Who's there?"

"A Friend with a friend," came the reply.

I lifted the bar from the door and opened it. A chill wind rushed in. On the other side of the door, in the deepness of the night, stood Jeremiah Strong and two others.

"Sister Spencer," he said. "Has thee room for wayfarers? They have come a long way."

"We've room and food as well," I said. "Come in. Welcome."

Two men entered the kitchen and stood silent, which was the usual way of things. The young Quaker stayed outside.

"Jeremiah, will you come in and take a bite of corn bread?"

He shook his head. "I must ride or the rising sun will catch me. God bless." He stepped off into the darkness.

I checked each window and drew the curtains tight, for I knew not what eyes watched the night. Then I hurried to feed the visitors.

The men wore ragged clothing. Their grateful smiles

and uninterrupted eating told me they were hungry. I sat beside the hearth and played with the low embers of the fire, so as not to seem to watch them eat. Curious as I was about where they'd come from and how, I asked no questions. This was Papa's rule, for the less we knew, the less we'd have to hide.

As they filled plates a second time I glanced toward the door and listened hard for sounds of pursuit. My heart thumped, its rhythm out of control. What dangers waited for these men outside our barred door and curtained windows? No. I dared not think such thoughts, for I still had work to do.

When they finished eating, I led them deep into the earth under our house, through the root cellar and into the hidden room. There they would pass the night in safety and comfort, for we always had blankets and straw pallets prepared.

The men would sleep well. They had run for days, perhaps weeks, with pursuers close behind. But I wouldn't sleep much. I never could. I climbed back into bed, and tossed this way and that. I hid my head under my pillow, but in my mind I heard the baying of hounds, saw their sharp teeth flash, felt myself running, always running, but never fast enough, never far enough.

In truth, excitement beats in my heart as strongly as fear—for I fancy myself a heroine, a woman of courage right out of the pages of one of Mr. Dickens's novels. So I sit here and write. I let my mind spin fearsome and bold pictures on these cold nights when, under cover of darkness, I fling the cloak of Moses around my shoulders and conduct the business of Egypt—freedom.

Sometimes I'm ashamed to be a Presbyterian. Drat the Reverend Cummings, anyway. He gives such spineless sermons, I'd doze even if I'd had a full night's sleep.

Lucky Mama. She and Tom stayed home today to guard our visitors. We told the church ladies she'd suffered a lowering of spirits, our usual excuse. It could be true, for Mama lost a baby last spring, and some women take a long time to recover. But Mama's cheeks are rosy and her chestnut hair glows in the firelight. I'm the one who looks pale and tired. I should have been allowed to miss services.

But then I'd have missed all the excitement.

I took the usual teasing on the ride to church. As I climbed up beside him, Papa boomed at me, "A slugabed again, daughter? Eating your breakfast on the wagon?" He winked and laughed, making crinkle lines around his eyes. "Fine wife you'll make someday."

"Jonathan Clark's wife?" Will asked. He sat in the hay behind Papa and me and kept hold of Miranda. "Tom and me have a nickel on when you'll marry him."

I turned to glare. He shook his head and grinned. Papa's grin on Mama's face: a wicked combination.

"A nickel?" Miranda asked. "Papa, may I have a nickel, too, when Lucy marries Jonathan Clark?"

My cheeks burned. "I haven't decided *if* I'll marry Jonathan, let alone *when*." But I did like him. And I'd see him soon.

The warm church welcomed us, and I loosened my

7

coat. We followed Papa up the aisle to our regular pew. Will's elbow poked my ribs when Jonathan stopped to say good morning.

"Look at them calf's eyes," Will whispered. "He's got it bad."

I smiled back at Jonathan and elbowed my brother. "Just you wait, Will Spencer. When you get sweet on some girl I'll torment you till kingdom come."

"Never," he said.

The organ called us to stand and sing. *A mighty fortress is our God, a bulwark never failing.* Miranda's high voice mingled with Papa's bass, and I felt surrounded by God's love and my family's.

Then another voice joined the singing. A fine, mellow tenor rose from the other side of Miranda.

I turned and saw a man at the end of our pew in Mama's usual place—a stranger with longish dark hair slicked back, wearing fancy gentleman's clothing. I listened as he sang and caught words that sounded unusual. *Power* came out "powah," *hate* sounded like "height."

The hymn ended. Miranda wriggled, and I reached into my pocket for a peppermint, a bribe to keep her still through the long service. The man caught my eye and smiled. And then he winked at me. In church! His eyes were the brightest blue.

Fire rose in my cheeks. Who was this man? He was way past twenty, too old for me to notice. But hard as I tried to pay attention to the sermon, my eyes returned to the handsome stranger.

As Reverend Cummings pronounced the benediction

the man slipped out the side aisle. When I reached the churchyard he was deep in conversation with several of the men. Papa and Will strode over to join them. Drat! If I were a boy, I could follow.

Miranda ran off to join a clutch of little girls spinning in their Sunday dresses. My dear friend Rebecca Carter took me by the arm and rescued me from the church ladies. She giggled and tossed her head, her bright gold hair afire in the sunlight. "Such a dull service. I'm in the mood for mischief," she said. "Remember the day we switched the privy signs behind the church?"

"Who could forget old Mrs. Cooper's face?" I grinned. "And what about the time we hid that bullfrog inside the pulpit? *Cr-roak. Cr-roak.* Let's plan something."

Rebecca laughed out loud. Her mother came up and tugged on her arm. "Father has the wagon ready. Have you giggled enough?"

"No!" we said together.

"You can't take her home." I pulled on Rebecca's other arm.

Her mother smiled. "I'd like to visit with your mother. You girls haven't had much time together since Christmas."

"We haven't. Please—come Wednesday for the midday meal."

Mrs. Carter steered Rebecca toward the waiting wagon. As I waved goodbye I caught the stranger's profile again. He lifted his blue eyes to me. He was talking to Papa. I itched to know who he was. I did better at pranks than patience.

"Good morning, Lucinda."

I pulled my attention away from the stranger. Jonathan Clark stood at my side.

"Lucinda?" He took my hand and squeezed it.

"I'm sorry, Jonathan—still humming that last hymn," I lied.

"Pa smells a January thaw. Ma wants a gathering before the blizzards hit and we get snowed in. The women will have a quilting bee, and the men will clear a piece of woodlot. Friday. Please come."

Jonathan looked at me with serious blue eyes, paler than the stranger's, I decided, but ready to smile if I said yes.

"Of course we'll come." A party was as good as a prank. Better!

Jonathan smiled, and his eyes lightened as if a cloud had passed by and gone. His plain, square face came alive, just for me.

I wished we weren't in the churchyard, surrounded by all our neighbors. If only we could ride off in Jonathan's wagon instead, and he could steal kisses . . . But Mama needed me at home this afternoon, worse luck.

I glanced again at the stranger. "Who is that man? He sat in Mama's place for the service."

"What? Do I have a rival, Lucinda? A tall, dark stranger?"

"Don't be silly. I can't be interested in him, he's too old." Another fib. And on a Sunday. For shame.

"Sorry, I don't know much," Jonathan said. He

shrugged. "I wanted to catch you before your pa got his team hitched." Jonathan hurried off to catch up with his parents, leaving me to wonder about the stranger.

Later at home, when Miranda was out of hearing, Papa shared what he'd discovered. "He's a Southern man. Asked for our help, as good Christians," Papa said. A scowl cut a harsh line across his face. "He's lost ten slaves and offers a thousand dollars for their recovery."

"A thousand dollars?" Mama asked. Her lips drew into a tight line. "That's the same as the penalty that hangs over Friend Whitman."

"That blasted law," Will said. "It's a crime against God and nature, that's what it is."

I agreed. "So much money!"

"The price of our whole farm," Papa said. "Times the twenty-six wild geese we helped last year alone. And two more now."

I can barely imagine the numbers. I can see the people easily enough. I remember every worried face. But the money. Tens of thousands of dollars. Fines like that would buy up our whole town.

And I had admired this handsome Southern man's smile! What in the name of Sunday was the matter with me?

SUNDAY, JANUARY 5, 1851
LATE EVENING

Waiting! I hate it. These nights are the worst. I think of runaways who travel across frozen fields, who wade through icy creeks to escape, and a shiver crawls up my spine.

It's late. Mama and I sit alone by the fire. Papa's out, driving our two visitors to the Quaker doctor in Ravenna, the next station. I write, or try to, while Mama rocks in her chair, her knitting needles clicking.

"Go on to bed, Lucinda. One of us should get some sleep."

"Please, Mama. Not till I know they're safe. Besides, I'd wake Miranda."

Mama nodded. "Catch an extra hour of sleep tomorrow, then. The washing won't take all day."

"Thank you, Mama."

"It's a blessing most of the travelers come now, when the rivers freeze over," Mama continued. "In the summer, with the crops and the garden, we're so busy."

"But we'll get busier still," I said. "That Fugitive Slave Act. More and more people will be coming north." I looked toward the window. Where was Papa? He should be home by now.

It wasn't always this difficult. At least, I don't remember such worries. Of course, Papa and Mama protected me from their activities at the beginning, when I was too young. They spoke of wild Canada geese. We still use those words as a code, to keep Miranda's ears from hearing things.

Mama and Papa have run a station from this house for nine years. Papa says God tugged on his conscience and sent him an abolitionist newspaper. It didn't occur to him to say no to God's call.

I've been helping since I was twelve, four years ago.

Will, thirteen, and now Tom, at nine, both join in, and it's a good thing, for so many more people are coming north.

I'd like to hide a bullfrog in President Fillmore's bed. He signed that dratted Fugitive Slave Act. God help us all. Used to be, free states were safe. Used to be, once a person crossed the Ohio River, he could change his name and disappear into a new life. No one could take him back south. Those days are gone now. Only Canada is safe. And for many, Ohio is the shortest route to Canada. We'll see more slaves, and more catchers too. I know it.

Poor Mama. Her forehead is creased and she rubs it and closes her eyes. We carry such worry around these days. We read stories in the newspapers of men put in jail back east for helping runaway slaves escape. And now our neighbor caught. Just the thought takes away my breath. It could happen to us.

MONDAY, JANUARY 6, 1851

Washing, washing, and more washing. My fingertips turn to prunes and then freeze when I clip the wet sheets to the line. It's so cold and dreary, I'm surprised the washing dries, but it does. Then we have to haul it all back inside. I'm too stiff for much writing tonight.

TUESDAY, JANUARY 7, 1851

Monday we wash, Tuesday we iron, week after week. What drudgery, especially in the winter. I'd happily trade a few wrinkled sheets for an afternoon with my books.

My Latin will fade unless I practice. *Amo, amas, amat.* Only half a week until Jonathan's party. Maybe the clouds will break on Friday.

WEDNESDAY, JANUARY 8, 1851

Bless Rebecca. The skies are still gray, but she's a beam of warm sunshine.

We baked molasses cookies and walnut bread for the party while our mothers sipped tea and gossiped. Of course, we sampled our sweets, too, and I'll not be ashamed to put my cooking in front of Jonathan's nose. His mother is another story. I hope she keeps her pointy nose elsewhere.

Please let our house stay quiet until Friday. No new geese. I couldn't bear to be left home as guard and miss the party. Selfish, I suppose, but the snows will come soon and we'll be housebound for a long time. I wonder why God created winter, anyway.

THURSDAY, JANUARY 9, 1851
EVENING

Tomorrow we'll drive to the party in two wagons, for Will has offered to haul the cut wood later. I helped him put fresh hay in one wagon bed this morning, so we'll ride warm and clean. When he's not making my life miserable with teasing he's not bad, for a brother. He's got a wagon of his own now and likes to haul goods for people.

"I'm in the transportation business," he bragged to me as he brushed his horses' manes.

I threw straw at him and stuffed some down his shirt.

He got me back with a huge armload, for he's taller than I am and strong from lifting goods into his wagon.

Drat it all. I get stuck at home washing and ironing while he gallivants across the countryside. I shouldn't complain—he worked hard for his wagon. He had it specially built with a false bottom by the Quakers in Salem. He uses it to carry folks north some nights, to spare Papa. Still, what I wouldn't give for a chance to ride off adventuring. I'd go anywhere—Cleveland, Columbus, even New York or Paris—if I could. If I didn't have all the chores.

This afternoon Miranda crawled into my lap, and the mood I was in, I made up stories for her about faraway places. "With our red hair, we might be related to those old-time Vikings," I began. "From the far, cold north, from the land of endless winter, came Prince Eric in search of the beautiful Princess Miranda. . . ."

After the tales, I made her practice her letters and her numbers until she grew too wriggly and jumped down.

"Lucy, what will we wear to the party tomorrow? Let's go see."

So I wasn't the only one excited. We raced for our room; I let her win. "Here, chickadee. Let's look at your fancy feathers."

"Oh, Lucy, you're so silly. Girls don't have feathers."

"Then what's this?" I asked, pulling her dress from its peg.

"My Sunday dress. It's my favorite. Did you have this dress when you were five?"

"Yes. It was my favorite, too." I'd loved the deep red velvet.

"I'm so glad you're my sister, Lucy," Miranda said. "We're just alike and we like the same dresses."

I swept her into my arms and swung her around and around. "We are wild Viking princesses, and tomorrow we shall visit the castle of the neighboring king. Perhaps we shall dance until morning and everyone will fall in love with us."

"Lucy, will you braid my hair? Will you make it fancy? A princess can't be plain."

"You'll never be plain, chickadee." I took a brush to Miranda's hair, rich russet waves that tumble down her back. Mama's hair. She passed the blazing color to all us children, like she passed on the pale skin and those dratted freckles that pop out every summer. But Miranda has waves, while my hair hangs straight.

"Lucy, will I be as pretty as you when I grow up? Will I have boys going sweet on me? I want to. I want to be just like you."

I hugged her then, tight as I could. We may be just farm princesses, but we have the best family in the world. And a party tomorrow! Bless Mr. and even Mrs. Clark for inviting us.

And Jonathan. God bless Jonathan Clark in particular.

My life has turned upside down.

Two days have passed, but it feels like two weeks. I'm not even at home. Tom and Will brought my things here this morning. People are sleeping now, so I can finally write everything down, but I fear it may take days for me to catch up with myself. And yet I must, for these two days have been more exciting than the rest of my life put together. What an adventure! And it has barely begun.

It all started quietly enough, but looking back, I should have suspected something right off. We'd no more than stepped inside the door to the Clarks' party when Charity Strong hurried up to me, her somber gray Quaker dress rustling. Her voice sounded cheery and calm as usual, but her dark eyes flashed me a warning. "Lucinda, I'm so glad to see thee. Here, let us collect the coats."

Though she's a Quaker and practices their plain life and odd, silent religion, she's a good friend. We went to school together. But more important, she's the sister of Jeremiah Strong, who brought the night visitors to our door just last Saturday, so I paid close attention.

When we reached the back bedroom Charity nudged the door shut with her foot. She sank to the bed and spoke in a quiet voice, her cheeks flushed. "Lucinda, my brother needs to speak with thee. Alone. It is most urgent. Many lives—"

The door opened, cutting off Charity's words and treating us to the spectacle of the Reverend's daughter.

Eleanora Cummings fussed with her curls and pinched her cheeks to redden them. Bah, who has time for that?

Many lives . . . Though my heart pounded, I spoke to Charity of ordinary things. "Will you sit with Rebecca and me? I'll never match your fine quilting stitches. Promise you won't notice. You're so patient and careful."

"A Quaker virtue, I'm told," she said, smiling. We left the room and she lowered her voice to a whisper. "My brother grows *im*patient, however. Thee will take supper with Jeremiah, please?"

"Yes. Of course."

Croaking bullfrogs, if I had known what I was getting into! I smiled and sat between Charity and Rebecca on the bench beside the quilting frame. Stretched before me was a quilt in shades of blue and green. I saw squares and triangles stitched in the pattern we call Wild Goose Chase. I suspected, from Charity's hints, that I would soon encounter more wild Canada geese!

Mrs. Clark studied my face with a knowing look. What was that about?

I itched to tell her what a perfect quilt she'd chosen that night. "A beautiful pattern," I said instead. "And the colors are strong."

Mama caught my eye. She understood about the geese.

Mrs. Clark, on the other hand, didn't understand at all. "I'm so glad you like it, Lucinda dear." She glowed.

Lucinda dear? Mrs. Clark had never called me that before. And the look on her bony face—pleased, as though she'd accomplished some purpose. That confused me.

Rebecca nudged me with her elbow. "It's a sign," she

whispered. Her cheeks reddened, and her eyes went soft and glowy. "Nathaniel Thatcher's mother has been nice to me lately, too. It's important that their mothers like us."

Important? Their mothers? Oh, no! Mrs. Clark had made the quilt with me in mind. Her son and me.

I squinted and held my needle up to the light for threading. My fingers shook, and it took me three tries to find the needle's eye. I like Jonathan Clark, more than like him. But I'm just sixteen. I'm not ready to let his mother stitch me into her pattern, not yet.

Girls on one side, women on the other, we sewed steadily for two hours. Mrs. Clark suggested a brief rest, and Rebecca, Charity, and I hurried outside, escaping the hard bench for fresh air and motion. We wandered toward the barn, where loud voices interrupted the bare quiet of a winter afternoon. Men and boys were loading split lengths of wood into Will's wagon. Jonathan Clark caught my eye and joined us.

"Lucinda, will you be my supper partner?"

"I'm sorry. Someone else has already asked. But I'd love to share a reel when the music starts."

He shrugged in a good-natured way and returned to the men.

Rebecca's eyes widened. Her pale eyebrows rose nearly to her hair. "Who already asked you?" she demanded. "What's going on?"

"Wait and see," I said. I winked at Charity.

Before we could return to the house, Nathaniel Thatcher asked Rebecca to be his partner. Matthew Brownell turned to Charity.

"Who, Lucy? Who?" Rebecca insisted when the boys had gone.

"I'm not telling." I grinned and spun around, twirling my skirt in a wide circle the way Miranda does, then ran back to the house.

If I had known then what I know now, would I have been so frivolous? Probably not. But then I would not have been able to act my role nearly so well, for I would have given everything away by being too serious. For it is serious business we undertake. *Many lives . . .*

SUNDAY, JANUARY 12, 1851
EARLY MORNING

No boring sermons this Sabbath! We're too busy cooking and washing up and toting armloads up and down the stairs. We have worked like threshers since Friday night.

In spite of the work, I find myself awake at night, filled with troubling thoughts. But then I remember the wild time we had at that party, perhaps the best prank I ever played. And who would have guessed it of the serious Quakers? I'll have to revise my opinion of them, and soon.

Jeremiah brought me supper at the party, as we had arranged. "Sister Spencer," he began.

"Jeremiah," I scolded, "you must call me Lucy."

He looked startled.

"And you might smile at me, if it's not too difficult. Otherwise people will wonder why we share supper."

He laughed aloud, and his solemn Quaker face turned

handsome, with dark eyes like Charity's. "I knew thee for a woman of courage," he said softly. "Thy humor is a surprise."

I heard a commotion to my left and turned. Charity, Rebecca, and their partners had just found seats and were looking in our direction. Jonathan Clark, with Eleanora Cummings at his side, stared at me, mouth agape like a freshly hooked fish.

I nodded to them all and turned back to Jeremiah, who had already cleaned much of his heaped plate. How do boys eat so fast?

"Have I caused thee trouble among thy friends?"

"Nothing I can't repair. Tell me, are you busy these days?" Inside I fumed, wishing we could talk freely.

"I fill my time," he said. "I help Father and Uncle with the inns, hauling firewood and supplies. I care for the horses, repair the wagons. What of thee, Lucinda? Surely farm work gets easier in winter."

"It does," I agreed. "I spend the hours of Miranda's nap in study, when Mama can spare me."

He smiled. "Still the student? What subjects?"

"Oh, Latin. Poetry and English literature just now." How could we talk calmly? I was so curious, I felt I might burst.

"No science? No nature studies?"

Ah! Bless Jeremiah. He'd given me the chance I needed.

"I find nature study difficult in winter," I began. "But we do watch the migrations of birds. Especially the wild Canada geese. Have you noticed? Birds fly north at odd times. Why, last week two males stopped over to rest and feed at our farm. I'm sure they've flown to Canada by now, though. They were strong and hardy."

"Strange. We've noticed the same pattern," he said. Jeremiah's eyes darkened until they seemed nearly black. The muscles of his face tightened. He tipped his head close to mine. "As we speak, my uncle shelters a flock. One bird is ill. We worry about their migration."

"How many?" I whispered.

"Nine to shelter, including the sick bird, and another in dire straits—ten in the flock altogether."

The number shocked me. We had taken care of small groups, threes and fours. But where would we put nine? And one was sick, another in dire straits—did that mean caught?

I suddenly remembered the handsome stranger from Sunday's church. The Southern man with ten slaves gone missing. It couldn't be just a coincidence.

I felt a tap on my shoulder and turned—Rebecca.

"Lucy, Jeremiah. What subject brings your heads so close together?" She sent me a look of pure mischief. "I didn't know you were so well acquainted."

Heat rose in my cheeks. What could I say?

"Lucinda and I share many common interests," Jeremiah replied, his voice calm and composed. "We both study Latin, literature, and nature. We are discussing the migration of birds."

Rebecca chuckled and tugged my braid. "You and I will talk later," she said to me. "The migration of birds, indeed!" She threaded her way back to her seat, still laughing.

My face burned.

"Thy cheeks are red, Lucinda. Thee might find a walk outside cooling."

"Yes, of course. I'd like a walk. It aids the digestion."

For shame! What a skilled liar I am. I had but one thought at that moment—escape from the barn. And so we did.

The wild geese rest again and I should too, but my fingers itch with the need to write this. Why is it that they always cramp up when I write out my Latin verbs, but I can scribble on forever when I have such news? Perhaps my heart drives my hand. For certainly Jeremiah is in my heart.

We escaped the barn and walked outside where two men tended a bonfire built from small branches and twigs left over from the woodcutting. Jeremiah led me to the far side of the fire, where snaps and hisses would guard our conversation from unfriendly ears.

I stood with my back to the fire to keep warm. "Nine people," I began. "Another in dire straits. It sounds serious."

"More than serious. The woman is with child. She nears her time and needs a rest."

"Nine people is so many. I'm not sure we have room for—"

"No. We have a different plan." He brushed his dark hair off his forehead. "Tonight, perhaps even now, thy brothers and their friends arrive at Sister Mercer's farm. She will be covered with spots, running a high fever. The boys will dump the load of wood and race back for help. I have warned Will and Thomas."

"Widow Mercer is ill?"

"Sister Mercer plays a part. Like thy family, she hasn't shouted her abolitionist opinions, so her farm is not suspect. She has room for many in her home and barns."

"A good plan," I agreed. "But it sounds like you need my brothers more than me."

"They will set the stage for our drama. Thee and the widow will play leading roles."

My heart thumped in anticipation. "What shall I do?"

"When thy brothers return, the boys will describe the spots—"

"Measles," I interrupted. "We've had them, Will, Tom, and I."

Jeremiah nodded. "My sister will offer to stay at Sister Mercer's house and help, but we Friends cause suspicion, for our beliefs are widely known. I'll remind Charity that she's not had the disease. Thee will rush in—"

"I'll say I've had the measles and offer to tend the widow."

"Charity and I will drive thee to the farm. Thy parents will agree?"

"I'm sure they will. I'll speak to Mama right away. The widow can't handle all those people alone."

"One thing more, Lucinda," Jeremiah began, but then he frowned. "Forgive me." Suddenly he bent and began to kiss me. His mouth felt soft on mine, his hands tightened at my shoulders.

My breath caught and my heart drummed. Jeremiah Strong was kissing me! I barely knew him!

My first instincts told me to pull away, but I held myself still for a moment, trying to understand. He wouldn't act so strangely without a reason. He had warned me first, but why?

Someone must be approaching. I reached up and put my arms around Jeremiah's neck, as if that were the most natural thing in the world.

His hands relaxed, and he held me warmly. He kissed me again, and I liked the feel of his lips on mine, soft, warm, gentle. Though I knew we were only pretending, my blood raced. I hugged him tight and kissed back. I liked his kissing. I didn't want it to be over.

Footsteps approached. We stepped apart. Jeremiah caught my hand as we turned toward the sound.

"So, Lucinda." Jonathan Clark glared at us, half his face lit by the fire, half in darkness. "Now I see why you refused to have supper with me."

His voice accused, and my temper flared like the bonfire. "Jeremiah asked me first," I said. "I was being courteous."

"Courteous?" Jonathan snapped. "I saw you just now, kissing this Quaker and enjoying it. And you." He turned to Jeremiah. "The Quaker girls don't like you, so you have to bother a Presbyterian? We don't mix with Quakers. Stick to your own kind, Strong."

"Surely all God's children are the same kind," Jeremiah replied.

I squeezed his hand. This was my fight, not his.

"Jonathan, please. I made a mistake. I'm sorry."

"You don't seem sorry," he said. A look of hurt crossed his face and his shoulders slumped. "Good night, Lucinda." He turned toward his house.

My heart was a lead weight. I cared for Jonathan, and my pretense had hurt him.

"I'm sorry, Lucinda," Jeremiah said. "Not for the kisses. I admit, I liked them." He smiled at me in the firelight. "But I dislike causing thee trouble."

There *would* be trouble. Jonathan had looked wounded. "He'll calm down." I hoped it was true. "I'll explain . . . I'll think of something."

I expected Jeremiah to drop my hand, but he didn't. He held it lightly. I liked the sensation, for the confrontation had shaken me. But the needs of the wayfarers tugged at my mind.

"You were saying something about the fugitives. Before . . ."

"So I was." His face sobered. "We have a serious problem. Catchers followed the runaways. One fugitive was captured—the only man. He cut off onto a side trail so that the catchers would chase him and we could carry the women and children to safety. We succeeded, but they caught him."

"Did you see the catchers? Was one tall, with long dark hair, slicked back?"

"We didn't see them. Why, do you know the man?"

"Maybe." I explained about the stranger who had taken Mama's seat in the church pew. "He lost ten slaves. He offered big rewards. Have they brought the captured man back south?"

"Not yet. They've taken him to Canton, to the magistrate there. Friends will try to free him from the jail and hurry him north. When we've hidden him safely, we'll bring the others and put them all on a steamship to Canada. But it could take time."

"Time?"

"Several days, perhaps a week. Could you manage that?"

"I'll stay as long as I'm needed—we could say Widow Mercer developed complications. Lung congestion, or dizziness."

"Thee won't mind?"

"Not at all."

He took my other hand in his and faced me. Firelight warmed his eyes. "I find much to admire in thee, Lucinda Spencer. I am glad to have thee on my side." He tipped my chin up with his thumb and kissed me again, this time lightly on the cheek. I felt a fluttering in my heart like the wings of birds.

I feel it now.

SUNDAY, JANUARY 12, 1851
EVENING

Even as I work long hours to help the runaways, I do so with only half my mind, for the other half lingers at that bonfire. I can still feel the soft warmth of Jeremiah's lips on mine. I touch my mouth again and again, to remember.

What's wrong with me? I consider myself in love with Jonathan Clark. Yet last week I let my eyes wander toward a handsome stranger who turns out to be a slaver. Now I can't forget the way Jeremiah Strong kissed me. No, that's not right. I haven't tried to forget. I remember every chance I get. What sort of girl behaves like that? A foolish one, I'm sure. And we have business to attend to, serious business. Perhaps once I write it all down, my mind will let it go and I can return to normal. I hope so.

Jeremiah's plan succeeded beyond all hopes. My brothers played their parts like actors in a traveling troupe. Even Mama helped without knowing exactly why. Bless her, for though she embarrassed me, it was the right thing to do.

She called me inside and scolded loudly. "Lucinda, your cheeks are flushed. Where have you been?" Heads turned.

"Please, Mama. People will overhear."

She marched me to an empty corner of the barn, the very picture of a mother angry with her misbehaving daughter.

She lowered her voice. "I'm sorry, Lucinda, but I assumed you must have news, since you had supper with the Quaker. People will leave us alone long enough for me to give you a good scolding."

I understood and held back a grin. Mama is a schemer, too. "Yes. Will and Tom should return any moment. They'll bring a story of Widow Mercer's illness. You must let me—"

I heard, in the distance, the creak of wagon wheels, the pounding of hoofbeats. We had no time.

Tom burst into the barn with a string of boys behind. "Mama, Papa! We found trouble at Widow Mercer's house."

"She's real sick," another boy said. "And the house is a mess."

"No apple pie," said the youngest Brownell boy. "No food at all, just dishes everywhere."

"She lay on the floor," Tom added. "All blazing hot and covered in spots, like when Will and Lucy and me got the measles."

I smiled to myself. Tom was wonderful. As he told his tale his freckles stood out on his pale, earnest face.

The barn had grown quiet when the boys arrived. Now a murmur arose. *Measles . . . dangerous for an older woman . . . measles . . . contagious . . .*

Will rushed inside and the room quieted again. "Mama, Papa, the widow's in bad shape. Her fire had nearly gone out. I built it back up. And once I saw those spots, I kept all the other boys out except Tom and me. But she needs help, bad."

Charity stepped toward Will, offering to help. She, Jeremiah, and I played our parts perfectly. Soon the noise rose again and people hurried to and fro. Mrs. Cummings and Mrs. Clark loaded a basket with food. Charity and I ran to the house for our coats. In no time Jeremiah hitched up his horses, people loaded food and blankets, and Papa was boosting Charity and me up into the wagon.

"I'll send your brothers tomorrow with your clothes," Papa said. "Take care of yourself, Lucinda. Tell Will if you need anything."

"Thank you, Papa." I hugged him and whispered in his ear, "Wild geese. Will and Tom will explain. I love you."

Jeremiah whipped up his team and we were off at a fast trot.

I turned to wave. Everyone, my family and all our friends and neighbors, waved and wished us well. I felt a tingle of conscience for lying to them. But it couldn't be helped. In that gathering, only the Spencers and the Strongs could know the truth.

Jonathan Clark stood apart and scowled as the wagon began to roll. I'd solve that problem later. For now, an adventure was under way. We'd pulled it off! And there I sat, so close to Jeremiah that his arm jostled me every time he lifted the reins.

He kept the pace until we were well beyond the Clark farm. Then he slowed the horses to a walk. "They'll have a long night," he said. "No reason to tire them out now."

I turned to face him. "Your plan worked. It was wonderful."

"Thank my sister," he said. "Charity invented the scheme. She'll tell thee the rest."

"Thee will help Sister Mercer prepare for the travelers," she told me. "Jeremiah and I will ride to Uncle's stables. I'll dress as a boy and drive the woman who is with child and her youngest in the closed trap. I'll come slowly with them. The rest we'll hide beneath the floorboards of this wagon, which Jeremiah will drive."

"You'll dress as a boy?" I'd done that, but a Quaker girl? "You always seemed so quiet and proper, Charity."

"Does thee think we Friends are all prunes? Dried up and boring? I always compose plots."

"And tangle me in most of them," Jeremiah complained, but he smiled. He took my hand and squeezed it lightly.

Charity glanced at our fingers, then smiled, too. "Jeremiah, Lucy, what have I started?"

My hand tingled and my heart thudded so hard, I thought surely they would hear. We weren't playacting. Jeremiah liked me enough to hold my hand in front of his sister and risk a teasing. I still pinch myself to make sure I haven't dreamed it all.

MONDAY, JANUARY 13, 1851

Widow Mercer—or Miss Aurelia, as I have agreed to call her—is a marvel. I always imagined her to be something of a recluse, sad and lonely. Well, she's not. She's full of spunk. She lives alone here in this great and elegant house and takes in nine secret guests as if that were the most natural thing in the world. Well, perhaps it is. Perhaps she's done this even more than we Spencers have.

I try to figure her out, but there aren't many clues. No, that's not right. She's really very frank and talks openly. I just don't know what to make of what I see and hear.

The first surprise came when she asked me to call her Aurelia.

"I couldn't. Mama would skin me alive. Would Mrs. Mercer be all right?"

She grinned at me, filled my arms with a pile of clean sheets, and pointed toward the stairs. "I haven't been a missus for years. Try Aurelia. You're full-grown."

"How about Miss Aurelia?"

She nodded. "All right. We're going up to the attic. I've got straw pallets there, and we'll spread them with sheets and blankets."

Miss Aurelia has a wonderful house—large, fancy too. Pictures hang everywhere and wood furniture shines with beeswax polish. The outside is grand, built with stone walls and lots of windows. It looks different from the other houses in our village, as though it was constructed all at once. Our house and most others started as log cabins and grew in a sprawl, a room or two at a time.

Miss Aurelia led me up to a back room with two beds. She pulled on a section of wood paneling next to the chimney and it swung out, revealing narrow, twisting steps. A secret door! She picked up a lantern and a stack of blankets and we climbed the steps.

The attic was warm and clean, and twice the size of the loft my brothers slept in at home. "You have space for twenty people up here," I said.

"I've had thirty, when pressed." She chuckled. "Imagine if the church ladies knew that. What would the good women say about poor old Widow Mercer then?" She shook out a sheet and tucked one end under the bottom of a straw pallet.

I followed her example. "I often wonder the same thing. We pretend that Mama's still feeling poorly about losing the baby when we need an excuse. It feels dishonest, but mostly it's exciting. I'm the one who gets up at night when needed."

I didn't know Aurelia Mercer all that well, but something about her manner loosened my tongue. I told her all about the scene with Will and Tom in the Clarks' barn. I kept the parts about Jeremiah and Jonathan to myself, though, for my feelings were still jumbled.

"I'd love to have seen it," she said. "Though I had fun lying on the floor while a troop of wild boys galloped through my house and shouted about measles. I nearly burst out laughing when that little Brownell boy went looking for apple pie. Have to bake those boys a few later, to thank them for my rescue." She laughed, a deep, hearty laugh that invited me to join right in.

"They said you were feverish, spotted. How did you do that?"

"Beets and whiskey."

"What?"

She stood and counted the made-up beds. "We've finished here. Come down to the kitchen. I do have pie hidden away, and I've put water on for tea. I'll disclose my secrets down there."

Several pots simmered on the cookstove and filled the kitchen with warmth and good smells. She fixed the tea, I cut the pie, and we sat at one end of a long cherrywood table to eat.

"Tell me about the beets and whiskey," I said.

"Well, first you must know that I'm not a drinking woman. But I keep a bottle of whiskey in the cupboard for coughs and croup."

"So does Mama," I said. "She doses us with whiskey and lemon. It burns going down, but the coughing stops."

"I've always had a strange reaction to strong spirits. A sip or two and my face turns red as a tomato. I get blazing hot all over."

"So your fever was whiskey?"

"Indeed. And for the spots I cut a beet in half, took a little twig, and painted my face and hands with dots of beet juice. Then, when I heard the boys' wagon, I swallowed two swigs of that vile liquor, stuck a clove in my mouth to cover the smell, and arranged myself on the floor like a near corpse. Sure didn't know if I could last without laughing. Lucky for me your brother Will scooted everybody else out when they decided I had the measles."

"They said your house was a mess. Dishes everywhere."

"Did you ever know a boy in your life who could tell dirty dishes from clean? I just spread things out before they came, and tucked them back in the cupboards when they left."

I looked around me. Not a sign of mess remained. "You should go on the stage," I said. "Who would have thought Widow Mercer could be so wicked?"

"Wicked indeed." She chuckled. "But I'll tell you this: Being grown doesn't have to make a person serious all the time. Our business is serious enough. God gave us laughter to ease our pains. He'd be disappointed if we forgot to use it. Even us old folks."

I couldn't see anything old about Miss Aurelia. She had no lines on her face, and her thick ash-brown hair had no sign of gray. I couldn't remember back to when her Mr. Mercer was alive. What a shame she was widowed young. She was so lovely. I wonder why she never remarried.

I dare not ask such personal questions. I'll get Mama to tell me more when I go home.

The clock over the hearth chimed, and I counted. Eight, nine, ten, eleven. "Will they arrive soon, do you think?"

"Midnight, I'd guess. Let me show you where you'll stay. I've given you the room right next door to me, so you can hear if this poor, sickly old woman takes a bad turn in the night. I've set out a nightgown, so you don't have to sleep all gussied up."

She laughed again, and I did too. I'd expected hard work, but I hadn't expected to feel so welcome and at home. I sent up a silent thanks that Jeremiah Strong had chosen me for this work. I had the feeling of stepping outside the ordinary, of embarking on the adventure of my life.

Jeremiah Strong. He's part of the adventure, too.

I sit here fiddling with my pen and run my thumb across my lips where he kissed me. When I look at the hand he held, a fire rises to my cheeks. I take a breath and try to calm my tumbling thoughts. Bah! It won't do for Miss Aurelia to catch me in such a mood. She'll think I've sampled her whiskey.

TUESDAY, JANUARY 14, 1851

Another day of hard work and gray skies. I'm not sure I remember what the sun looks like.

Our visitors seem to have caught up with themselves at last. Saturday, Sunday, and Monday all they did was sleep and eat. Until today they had no time, nor energy, for conversation. No wonder, considering how thin and cold and ragged they looked when they arrived. But they have rested some.

I wish I could say the same. My mind still whirls like a summer tornado. The visitors—six children, one baby, and two women—keep us busy enough to tire me out, cooking, washing up, and carrying. And then I have the barn chores. But between worry about the danger and excitement about the adventure, I still find it difficult to get a whole night's sleep.

Also, since the fugitives have been awake more today, I've begun to tie names to faces. There's a woman named Emma. Now that she's regained some strength, we've talked. I try to remember Papa's rule and not ask questions, but Emma's not shy.

She was ready for conversation this morning when we carried up breakfast. "Ben, Shad, Naomi, Daniel, sit yourselves up straight," she said to four little ones. "Say good morning to Miss Lucy."

The children looked at me and nodded but didn't say anything.

"Over there be Ruth and Mesha." She pointed toward a small girl and a tiny boy. "They Cass's babies. And this hungry gal, she my Lizzie." She held a sturdy child to her breast.

"You're feeling better? Rested now?"

"Some better. Can't help but worry, though. My Abraham, he got himself caught to save the rest of us."

I didn't know what to say to that. So I bit my lip and changed the subject. "Is Cass feeling better, too?" I looked toward the bed where she lay, still sleeping.

Emma lifted the milk pitcher with her free hand. She

looked at me over the children's heads and shook her head.

I worried about Cass. She looked terrible. She had medium brown skin, but behind the brown, her face looked gray and sickly. Pain lines furrowed her puffy skin.

Seeing Cass brought back bad memories for me. It carried me back to those days last spring when Mama just lay there, still and quiet. Of course, she had her reasons. She'd lost a child in the birthing bed. But at times I wondered if she was lost to us as well. Thank the good Lord she came back. I'll pray for Cass and ask God to heal her as He healed my mama. Surely He will hear me.

WEDNESDAY, JANUARY 15, 1851

Bless Thomas! He and Will brought a few essentials for me on Saturday, but today he made another trip with his wagon piled high—more food, outgrown clothes Mama sent for the young guests, and the rest of my clothes, books, and sewing things in two big boxes. After unpacking all that, I feel I have moved into Miss Aurelia's fine house. My clothes have never hung in such a beautiful walnut wardrobe.

Best of all, Tom brought me letters. I have read them three times each and will fold them into my journal to keep. And after reading them once more, I'll have to find a safe place to hide my journal, for Papa's words remind me of the caution I must always exercise. I have been lax. Dangerously so.

14 *January*

Dear Lucinda,

Your brothers have told us more of Widow Mercer's illness. Sadly, it is a spreading sickness that keeps you from your home for the coming days. You are a brave girl to fight against it until this terrible disease is cured. I thank God daily that my family is strong and in good health. I am proud of each one of you and the parts you play.

I would take your place and care for Widow Mercer myself if I could, but that wouldn't be seemly. I pray you will use extreme caution and not be caught by some stray contagion. Keep vigilant. Do not take the slightest chance. You carry life in your hands. Do not lose yourself in daydreaming, else you slip. I pray God will watch over you and your charge. You are in our hearts.

Love,
Papa

14 *January*

Darling Lucy,

Your father and I are so proud of you. We miss you, of course. But we'll have you back soon, and full of tales, if I'm not mistaken. You will miss some of the Reverend Cummings's inspiring sermons, which I'm sure weighs down your heart. Don't worry. He'll let you read them if you but ask.

Dear girl, take care of yourself and your charge. Be useful to Aurelia Mercer. She is a good woman, if a bit unusual. Your papa has written his cautions, so I won't overburden you *with mine. Just know that we both send our love and our prayers your way.*

With a hug and kiss,
Mama

I read my parents' letters yet again and I hold my arms close to my chest and hug myself. My eyes fill. Already I miss Mama's hugs, her humor, her spirit. I've never been away from home before. How will I get along for a week without her?

And Papa. I've never heard him so serious, so fearsome. The fact that he writes in code sobers me. And he warns about being caught by some stray contagion. That word again. *Caught.* I can't help but recall that stranger in church. Oh, how I wish I were home.

As I write this a tear dampens my cheek. I brush it away, ashamed. Here I sit only a few miles from my home and I feel lost. How much harder it must be for the families we shelter. They left everyone and everything behind. And one was captured. My family is whole and safe and nearby.

I'll read Miranda's words again. Surely they'll cheer me.

Dear Lucy,
Mama says she'll write what I say. I want to come, too. I want to help with the measles.
Mama says the measles are itchy and hot, but I don't care. I miss you and miss you.
I have a new friend. Reddie is a redbird and his wing is

_____

hurt. We keep him in a box in the loft so Brutus won't eat him for supper. Shame on Brutus. Bad cat.

Reddie misses you, too. But he likes eating your corn bread.

Mama says I must help Reddie get well while you help Widow Mercer get well. That's what I will do.

Come home soon, soon, soon.

Love,
Miranda

Miranda and her precious animals. She has a soft heart and a gentle hand. It won't be long before she'll help rescue people as well as wild animals. In another five years, perhaps . . .

But no. I don't want to think so far ahead. Perhaps in five years there will no longer be a need for us to do this work. In five years I might be permanently gone from my home. I might be married and have children of my own. With that thought, I unfold the letter from Jonathan Clark. Drat it all, I am so confused.

11 *January*

My dear Lucinda,

I'm sorry I got so upset last evening. I spent the whole night in thought about what happened and I still don't understand. I'd come and speak with you, but Ma won't allow it. She's afraid I'll get the measles. Sometimes Ma forgets that I'm a man, or nearly. She treats me like a child. Since I can't come, I've decided to write. I hope your brother will deliver this promptly and that you will reply.

As I said, I stayed up all night. Remember the hill at the far northeastern corner of our farm? Where the creek pools up below and we swim all summer? That's my favorite place. There's a big flat rock where I climb up and think about things. We picnicked there last summer, do you remember? I haven't forgotten. It was the first time we kissed.

Last night I took a couple of horse blankets and lay on the rock to study the stars and ponder.

And here's what I think: I haven't made my feelings clear to you. I haven't asked you to share yours.

I care for you, Lucinda. I can't imagine my life without you in the center. But since I haven't been bold enough to tell you, perhaps you haven't understood. Is that it? Did you allow that Quaker to kiss you because you didn't know of my affection? Because you thought my kisses were only childish games? If so, I'll forgive you. Indeed, I'll need to forgive myself, for it is more my fault than yours. Know this, Lucinda. A man's heart beats in my chest—it beats for you.

Another thought came to me. Did you even allow the kiss I saw? If that Quaker forced you, just say the word and I'll make him sorrier than he's ever been. I've never thought much of those Quakers, with their silent services and stern faces. I think they keep secrets under those round hats.

One more question I must ask, even if it hurts. Have I misjudged your feelings? Do you like him more than you like me? If so, and I pray it isn't so, please write and tell me straight out. I will take as a man whatever comes.

I hope my thoughts, jumbled as they are, haven't over-burdened you. I know you are an angel, caring for a sick *neighbor. It is one of the many reasons I cherish you, my dear Lucinda.*

Yours,
Jonathan

A big sigh escapes as I finish reading. Every time I read this letter his words warm and trouble me. I do feel cherished, but confused, too.

If only Mama were here to tell me what to do. But she isn't, so I must tuck all my letters into this journal and hide the whole business deep in my box of soiled clothing.

I don't expect Miss Aurelia to snoop in my belongings, but if she somehow found my private thoughts, I'd be greatly embarrassed. And if somebody else found them, the wrong somebody, disaster would strike.

THURSDAY, JANUARY 16, 1851

January is half gone and still no sign of the sun. And the clouds today seem grayer than ever. Is this possible? Of course it's possible; winter in northern Ohio is bleak at best. Now I fear we are about to get its worst.

Dear Thomas. He's such a good boy. Yesterday before he left he stacked all the new-cut wood for Miss Aurelia. He carried lots of it to the back porch for us, and a good thing, too. If those aren't snow clouds I see piling up in the western sky, I'm a dappled mare.

And speaking of the mare, I must string a rope from the house to the barn so that if the snows do come, we won't lose our way when we feed the horses and do the milking. Just in case . . .

I am no dappled mare.

Snow came in the night while we were sleeping. Up in the attic the baby cried, as she does some nights. It woke me and I listened, wondering if I'd be needed. I heard footsteps, her mother tending her, and then no more cries. No sounds at all, just a deep silence, as if I lay in a room filled with pillows. I crept from my bed and peered out. The clouds had emptied their treasures for us, billowing drifts of white diamonds. The first snow of the new year.

I tiptoed downstairs and made for the front door. I pushed it open to touch the snow, to taste the cold, sharp cleanness with my tongue. As I pushed, something fell from the door, as if wedged there. I bent to pick it up. A letter. I brushed snow off the paper before it could melt and cause the ink to run.

I allowed myself only a moment to savor the white world, then hurried to the kitchen and poked up the fire, added a log, and fanned it into flame. I held the letter to the light and saw my name. I didn't recognize the handwriting.

Dear Lucinda,

Nearly a week has passed since last I saw thee. Every day thoughts tumble about in my mind, running every which way like children playing at tag. I've tried to write, but each time I burn the letter. This time I will not burn it, but rather I will share all my thoughts and thee must make of them what thee will. Sort them and choose which is wheat, which is chaff. I am at thy mercy.

To begin, I beg forgiveness for my first, impetuous kiss. I hope thee understands that I was driven to it. I could not help myself. I hope I did not offend.

There, that's said. I hope thee wears a smile on thy face and remembers the kiss with fondness, for though I had not intended it, I do not regret it. If I must tell the truth (and we Friends require that of ourselves always), having tasted one kiss, I wish I had stolen many more. Given the chance, I shall do just that. But that is for thee to decide. And if the clouds bring snow, as it seems they will, thee will have much time for thy deliberations.

If indeed the snow comes, I shall try a winter's journey, for I've a fondness for travel by sleigh. One can drive for miles without seeing a soul, and the falling snow and wind erase one's tracks and make the ground new again. There are joys in such a journey, for me at least. Especially these days. But I'll be cautious in my adventures, I'll carry wagon wheels along in case the snow melts before my journey is successful.

Pray that I will succeed, dear Lucinda, for there is always risk with winter travel. I hope to return before the coming snow has melted, and if thy heart is so inclined, perhaps I'll find a reply to my letter.

Do write to me, and have a care for thyself. Watch over thy charge, for Sister Mercer depends on thee. I believe she is in the best of hands, and when I return, perhaps thy burden shall be lightened, God willing. And may God bless thee and watch over thee.

Thy admiring Friend,
Jeremiah Strong

Jeremiah.

Who would have thought such warm words could come from him? He is as affected as I. I've read the letter over and over. The words are scribed in my heart, so I barely need the page, but I will keep it, of course, under my pillow. He writes so cleverly, he places no one at risk. Except himself as he travels.

Jeremiah does make me laugh. I am not such a siren that men fall at my feet and fling kisses upon me at every turn. Why, if Jeremiah was driven by the fires of love to kiss me, he's had chance after chance, for he's made many a trip to my door late at night. But . . .

He wants to kiss me again. I close my eyes and see his dark hair and dark eyes, the way his cheeks redden with the cold or when he has fervent feelings about something . . . And he has fervent feelings about me!

Bless the winter, bless the snow, bless the measles and Miss Aurelia and all the wild geese who have drawn us together.

Jeremiah.

Jeremiah.
Jeremiah Strong.

I am still no dappled mare. It has snowed and snowed, drifted and blown and whirled until the whole landscape glows white in the dim light. How I got through this day I'll never know, for I kept Jeremiah's letter tucked inside my pocket and patted it every other moment. Surely Miss Aurelia and Emma suspected something. But perhaps they blamed it on the snow. It made me a little reckless.

"A spell of snow won't hurt," Miss Aurelia said as she came downstairs at first light. "We've got plenty of food and firewood." She frowned. "But it will slow things down."

"How do you mean?"

"Emma's husband, Abraham. They're holding him in custody in Canton. The Quakers plan to spring him from jail, but the snow will hinder them as well. He must be mightily worried about his family—as they are about him. Just hope young Mr. Strong gets him out safely."

"I think the snow may help the rescue instead of hinder. I've received a letter." I touched my pocket. "Jeremiah plans a trip with a sleigh, a winter's journey. He says the snow and wind will erase his tracks, and he asks us to pray for his success. What else could he mean?"

Miss Aurelia nodded. "Brave young man, that Quaker. It's a full-blown blizzard out there. I'd not choose to be about in it."

"I believe he left yesterday, so perhaps he's near to Canton by now." A shiver went up my back as I thought of Jeremiah, somewhere on a winding road with a storm blowing. And that dratted Southern slaver on the prowl. Blow, wind, blow hard. Cover the tracks of the sleigh. "Please, God, keep him safe," I whispered.

Miss Aurelia smiled at me and put her arm around my shoulder. "Amen," she said. "Keep us all safe."

We cooked a hearty breakfast of flapjacks and sausages and hauled it up to the attic. But our guests peered out the windows instead of sitting to eat.

"Snow. Mama say this here's snow." Ben, the oldest boy, pointed and shook his head at me in wonder. It was the most he'd said to me so far—the children seemed wary of me. In truth, I'd had very little real conversation with any of our visitors, for though I talked some with Emma, she spent more time with Miss Aurelia, and Cass was too unwell to do much but lie in bed.

I rubbed at the window so we could see better. "You've never seen snow before?"

"Nope. Our place, it be warm. We get rain but no snow."

"You wait," I said. "You'll see lots of snow in Canada."

"What it feel like?"

"If you eat all your breakfast, I'll see what I can do," I promised. "Maybe we can go outside."

But Miss Aurelia said no. "It's too risky."

"Please! The children have never seen snow. And they've been cooped up in the attic nearly a week."

She put her arm around my shoulder. "Lucinda, dear,

what you say is true. They have been cooped up. But they have also been *safe.* We mustn't endanger them. Remember, if the Quakers can get through the snow to save their father, the catchers can also get through. We must be vigilant, dear child, no matter how boring it grows."

I looked down. A scolding was still a scolding, even when kindly put. And I deserved every word. "I'm sorry. I wasn't thinking straight. I get excited when it snows. I—"

"You're a young girl. I've counted on your strong legs and willing arms to carry food and supplies upstairs day after day. Now you must count on me to make wise choices. Let's open that trunk of outgrown clothes and get out our sewing baskets. I'd like to send our guests on to Canada with warm, well-mended clothing. With you, Emma, and me stitching, the work will go fast enough."

She was right, of course. And so we stitched and hemmed and remade garments that my brothers and sister had outgrown. We talked a little as we worked, but I sensed that Emma's thoughts were with Abraham. And I understood, for I thought constantly of Jeremiah and dreamed that I journeyed with him, out in the snow, with no one to follow the tracks of our sleigh.

SATURDAY, JANUARY 18, 1851
EARLY MORNING

I hope this snow is falling on President Fillmore. And I hope someone makes him stay inside, too, and doesn't allow him to make a single snow angel or throw a single snowball. Bah on all the politicians!

How long will it take Jeremiah to travel to Canton and

back? Two days each way, four days total in good weather. But I must allow for the snow. And he and the others will need time to break Abraham out of jail. Will five days be enough? I surely hope so. But I should probably expect him to be gone at least six. If he left sometime on Thursday, he could return by Monday or Tuesday. How will I fill my time until then? With stitching, I guess, and more work. And letters too. Since we're snowbound, I'll write to everyone. But I'll have to be careful. I too will have to write some thoughts in code.

18 *January*

Dear Mama and Papa,

As I sit here and tend to Widow Mercer on this snowy afternoon, I thank you for sending the letters, my books, and the dried-apple pies you baked, Mama. They disappeared quite rapidly. Your fine cooking would make anyone feel better.

Miss Aurelia, as she insists I call her, is a clever woman. I am working at the box of mending you sent, and she had the best idea. Since you sewed William several pairs of trousers from the same cloth, I am taking each pair apart. Will wore out the knees of every pair, ruining the fronts. Miss Aurelia said why not sew the undamaged backs together for a new pair of trousers? They look fine this way and should hold up much better than repeated patches.

As you may gather, I keep quite busy. Mama, tending a house is more work than I'd realized. Papa, tell Will and Tom that I also milk and tend to Miss Aurelia's horses, but if the snow lets up, I will surely invite their help.

Dear Miranda, your new friend, Reddie, sounds quite

beautiful. I too hope he is well and flying again when I return, for I shall want my share of corn bread back. You have given him a rather ordinary name, however. Had you thought of Horatio? Prince Hal? Tell him "Peep, peep" for me. That's "hello" in redbird.

Isn't the snow beautiful? I yearn to be outside in it, but Miss Aurelia needs me to stay inside, and so I shall. With such illness abroad in the land, safety and caution must come first. You were right to advise me, Papa.

But don't worry, for I am young and healthy and strong. And I know how to look out for myself. Do you realize that I've been away from home for a week? I manage better than I might have expected. Perhaps it is because I'm so busy. Or else maybe I'm growing up. I do miss you all, though. I treasure my brothers' visits and look forward to returning home soon.

May God keep you in His care.

Your loving daughter,
Lucinda

18 January

Dear Rebecca,

I'm so confused. When the snow melts and my duty here is done, we must visit. I'll fill your ears with news for two days. Just now I write for guidance. I know you won't receive this letter before I must decide, but if I pretend to talk with you as I write, perhaps I'll hear your advice in my mind. I surely need someone, and I don't know Miss Aurelia well enough. And she's Mama's age and may not remember what it feels like to be young and in love.

Yes, Rebecca, in love. You must promise to seal my secrets

deep in your heart and press a large lump of wax over the edges, as they did in the old days of kings and queens.

I know we've talked of this before. But Rebecca, I'm so unsure. Who am I supposed to love? Jonathan Clark? He began kissing me last summer, sweet and gentle kisses. Our romance grew through the fall. Sunday afternoons we'd go for drives in his wagon. With his arm around my waist, with all those kisses, I burned like August in November. I could barely sit through the Reverend's sermons for thoughts of what the afternoon would bring. Oh, Rebecca! Am I wicked? Surely you feel the same way about Nathaniel. Surely God intends us to love one another. He says as much in the Bible.

I am wicked. I admit it. For I love two boys at once. It began at the party. Until then, Jeremiah Strong was just some-one I knew. Yes, Jeremiah! Charity's older brother, too mature for me and a Quaker as well. Oh, Rebecca, he kissed me. And I liked it. What I said before was wrong—he's not a boy like Jonathan. He's a man. A lovely man. I wanted him to kiss me again.

I've thought of him every minute since Friday. But what will the church ladies think? The townspeople? Quakers and Presbyterians do not fall in love, do they? We are so different, and we mostly keep to our own.

But is that God's choice or ours? For surely we all worship the same God. We are all His children, even if we speak to Him in different ways. If I liked the Reverend Cummings better, I would ask him my questions, but he is such a dry little man. I don't want his boring opinions.

What I wonder is this: If I do love Jeremiah, and if he loves me, and if somehow we are intended to care for each other . . . well, drat it all, Rebecca, will I have to turn into a

Quaker? I dearly hope not, for I can't bear the drabness of gray dresses.

And yet inside that sober gray suit of his, Jeremiah has a heart that is warm and golden. What shall I do?

Yours perplexedly,
Lucinda

SATURDAY, JANUARY 18, 1851
EVENING

Snow and more snow. Stitching and more stitching. Will it ever end? We did something nice today, though. The children have grown ever more restless with staying quiet in the attic. And I've been itching to play in the snow. So I carried a washtub of snow up the stairs, Miss Aurelia heated maple syrup, and we made snow candy. I lay on the floor and pretended it was snow to teach the children about snow angels, and showed them how to make snowballs. We took our snowballs, lined them up inside the washtub, and made a miniature snow fort. It was the first time the children seemed to lose their fear of me, and I loved it—just playing together. Even Cass sat up and smiled.

As I carried the tub of melting snow downstairs I felt a heavy sadness inside. This tub was a poor substitute for real play. But when Abraham is finally freed and they can travel to Canada, they will at least know how to enjoy snow. Two more days until that happens, by my calculations.

In the afternoon Cass and the children rested. Emma, Miss Aurelia, and I sat near the attic windows to sew. As we stitched, Emma and I also got to know each other a little, for despite Papa's rule, I couldn't swallow all my questions. Our visitors were warming to us. Should I harden my heart? Papa might say yes, but Papa isn't here.

"Did you come a long way?" I asked as I hemmed a shirt.

"We come from Carolina," Emma told us. "Take a lot of nights walking to get here."

I looked over to the bed where Cass dozed. "It must have been hard, with the children and with Cass sick. Is she feeling better yet?" Emma and Miss Aurelia spend more time tending Cass than I do. I mostly haul things up and down the stairs.

"She resting a lot."

I bit my bottom lip. "How long do you think? Until she has the baby, I mean. Will she get better after that?" Papa would scowl at my questions, but Miss Aurelia just sat up a little straighter and listened, like she was glad I'd asked.

Emma frowned. "Month or two, I guess. I hope she get better sooner, so we can get north 'fore the child come."

"I hope so too. I'm praying for her. For all of you. And Abraham."

Emma nodded. But the mention of Abraham seemed to take her back into her own thoughts. And so we just sat and stitched.

We held services this morning, and they were much finer than any I've heard lately in the Presbyterian church. We began with hymns. Miss Aurelia and I sang "A Mighty Fortress." Emma and the children shared one called "Climbing Up the Mountain." We sang "He Walks with Me and He Talks with Me." They sang "Swing Low, Sweet Chariot." The songs went on for quite a while as we tried to teach each other the tunes and the words. The music seemed to comfort Cass, for she sat up and sang along in a low, sweet voice.

Emma ended by singing a real slow song all by herself, "Steal Away to Jesus." I liked it a lot, for that's what we do, help the fugitives steal away. And I figure Jesus is on our side in the matter.

After we sang, Miss Aurelia got out her Bible. Before she could even open the pages, the children began to clamor for stories.

"Tell my story," Naomi said. "Mine and Ruth's."

"No, mine," Daniel insisted. He raised his hands, pawed the air, and roared at me like a wild lion cub.

Daniel in the lion's den. Naomi and Ruth's promise of lifelong devotion.

The older children decided the order of the stories.

"Me and Shad be the biggest, so we be first," Ben said. He smiled at me as though he expected me to understand.

"Your names come from the Bible, too?" I asked, puzzled.

He nodded. "Shadrach, Meshach, and Abednego. That Shad, Mesha, and me."

"Oh! My brothers like that story, too," I said. "It's scary."

Miss Aurelia found the right pages and began to read. "Nebuchadnezzer the king made an image of gold whose height was threescore cubits, and the breadth thereof six cubits: he set it up in the plain of Dura. . . ."

I knew this story. But never before had I understood its true meaning. God loved all his children, and he would deliver them from harm, from a fiery furnace, from a lion's den. Emma and Cass had named their children in the faith that God would deliver them from the evil bonds of slavery.

I prayed that deliverance would come soon.

Miss Aurelia read from the Book of Ruth—in the place where Ruth is told to return to her homeland, but she refuses. "And Ruth said, 'Intreat me not to leave thee, or to return from following after thee; for whither thou goest, I will go; and where thou lodgest, I will lodge. . . .' "

Naomi took Ruth's little hand and said, "I be your people."

Ruth nodded. "I be your people, too. I go where you go."

I could barely listen. My throat thickened and my eyes fogged. I'd thought myself educated. I'd thought myself a serious thinker and a strong Christian. But looking at those two little girls who held tight to each other's hands, I realized they'd traveled miles and miles ahead of me.

Dear Lord, I still have a long way to go.

I have tried to write a letter to Jonathan. My conscience nips. I must write him, for we have liked each other a very long time. Yet I can't find the words. To be completely honest, I also can't quite find the affection I ought to have for him. I try to imagine his face, but dark eyes replace blue ones in my mind.

And so I dawdle and chew on my pen. Am I a coward? Flighty? Probably. So be it. Once this adventure is finished, surely I'll settle down and return to my usual self. My heart will remember Jonathan, and we will go forward together. But just now I'll write to Jeremiah instead.

19 *January*

Dear Jeremiah,

Your letter brought a smile to my face. Who would have thought that our common love of nature studies, and in particular our interest in the migration of birds, would lead to kisses?

Rest assured you did not offend me with your attentions. I'll admit you startled me, but I am a girl who likes surprises. I will not be sorry if you should choose to surprise me again.

In the meantime, between snow and chores and caring for my responsibilities, I keep quite busy. But not so busy I haven't wondered about your journey. Was it successful? Did you voyage into a sea of snow like some long-ago explorer? I think of you often as the wind blows and the drifts grow ever taller. I hope you will return tomorrow, with news perhaps, and share your adventures with me.

Just a word about our common interest—I have watched the skies but seen neither beak nor feather, neither goose nor hawk. Even the birds are deep in hiding from the storm, safe and warm, in their own nests, perhaps, or in borrowed ones. I hope you are likewise, safe and warm, or that soon you will be. I also pray that God will remind the sun to shine upon us so that all His creatures may again walk, run, swim, or fly, freely, to their destinations.

Your bird-watching friend,
Lucinda

MONDAY, JANUARY 20, 1851

The calendar will say otherwise, but for me today was the longest day in the year. I waited and watched, but Jeremiah never came. He sent no messages. I found no letter wedged in the door, although I looked several times.

What is happening? Has he been caught, like Friend Whitman? Or did the storm stop the rescue? Is he in danger from magistrates and catchers, or from the same storm that blows snow against the barn in ten-foot drifts? I can't bear to think about either possibility, but danger has haunted me all day long.

Still, chores must get done. Miss Aurelia and I washed a week's worth of clothing for ourselves and our visitors. With the weather so bad, I hung the wet laundry in the attic, where a clothesline is strung at one end. Emma pegged up the clothes with me, which helped a great deal, for there was twice the load Mama and I usually wrestle with. We hummed our hymn tunes softly, but by the end of the day, hymns or no, my fingers were raw, and my heart was too.

TUESDAY, JANUARY 21, 1851

Still no news of Jeremiah, nor any sunshine. The snow has stopped, at least, but clouds remain and cast gray shadows in my heart. I hefted the heated flatiron today with the force of my worries, and if the cloth could speak, it might have said, "Ouch, don't pound on me."

WEDNESDAY, JANUARY 22, 1851

I have learned so much today that my mind has less room for worry—at least about Jeremiah, though I do wonder if he cares for me, since he has sent no messages. Bah!

We sat by the attic window again today and stitched. I sewed on a blue dress for little Ruth. Emma needed some thread.

"Miss Lucy, will you pass me some black thread?"

"Sure, Emma. But why do you call me Miss Lucy?"

"The children, they trained to call grown people Mister or Miss. It be proper. Show respect."

"But you're older than I am. I should call you Miss Emma."

"You white. I colored. The rules be different. But I not so old," she said with a laugh. "I about twenty-four, twenty-five, something like that. My sister, Cass, she about nineteen."

Sisters! What a dunce I am. I missed all the clues.

Cass is so heavy with child that I failed to notice the similarities—both women are tall, with strong, wide cheekbones, deep-set eyes, rich brown skin.

Emma seems old, thirty or more. And Cass is just three years older than I am. Impossible.

I looked over to the pallet where Cass lay, dozing. Papa's rule buzzed in my ear, but I ignored it.

"If you don't mind me asking, what's wrong with Cass? What I don't know about birthing babies would fill a whole shelf of books."

"Her legs. They swell up. She got to lie down till the child come. Then she be herself again."

"Does that happen often?" Miss Aurelia asked. She pulled her chair close to Emma and me. "I haven't often seen a woman close to her time."

Now isn't that a pickle? Miss Aurelia and I are both ignorant about babies. Great help we'll be if Cass starts having her baby here. But she won't start yet, will she? Surely she'll wait until Abraham gets free and they go to Canada. I'm counting on that. Besides, Emma's here. Emma knows what to do. She'll take charge.

"It happen," Emma continued, as we stitched up in the attic. "Cass, she swell up every baby. I never do. Too bad she have to come north when she so far gone."

Far gone—that sounded bad. "Did something make you hurry?"

"You might say. Abraham and me, we talk. Our boys grow big enough to work like men. That mean they grow big enough to get sold. So we plan to cut and run when spring come—after Cass birth her baby and mend awhile. But that Missy Roberts, she wicked. The master gone a-travelin' and the wife, she decide to get rid of Cass. One of the cooking gals hear about it. So we run, every one of us, swelled-up legs or no."

"The master's wife planned to sell Cass?" Miss Aurelia asked. She frowned. "Has that happened before to your family?"

"Oh, yes. Cass, she all I got left. Our mama die. Our daddy, our brothers, they long gone. Sold south. Master, he keep Cass and me to breed. We grow new slaves for him, so he keep us and sell off the rest."

To breed? The word exploded in my mind. We'd heard tales of families separated and sold apart, but breeding? That word was meant for livestock—not people. Did Mama and Papa know about this? I needed to understand. "Did Cass's man get sold, too?"

Emma snorted. "Cass ain't got no man. She ain't allowed to have no man. Any man look at Cass, he get a taste of that cowskin."

"But . . ."

"Ain't you studied little Ruth? Mesha? They be mighty pale."

The truth hit me with a whoosh, a heap of snow sliding off the roof. The master. Cass's children were *his* children. And of course his white wife would have gotten rid of Cass while he traveled. Out of wretched jealousy, she'd have sold Cass and broken up the tiny remnant of family the two sisters had saved.

My breakfast felt heavy and sour in my stomach. I took Emma's hand. "I'm sorry. I had no business asking."

"You got no reason for sorry, Miss Lucy," she said. "The good people must know what happen down south if they going to stop it." She stabbed her needle in and out of the trousers she held.

She's right. But the knowledge frightens me. Now I understand why that awful slaver chased after them in such a hurry. He's lost ten slaves. One was his mistress, two others his own children.

Poor Cass. She's my age, or close to it. I have two young men I like, and the time and freedom to choose one. She has no choices at all. Just a master. An owner. Try as I might, I can't get these hard words out of my mind.

"You all right, Lucinda?" Miss Aurelia had asked. She'd put her hand on my forehead, testing for a fever.

"I'll be fine," I said.

I lied, of course.

I can't imagine ever being fine again. The notion that people not only *own* other people but use and misuse them however they wish—it's evil. I sit here and shiver. The skin on my back ripples, like a hundred spiders are crawling on it.

And then another thought comes. I saw this man, their master, in church. He winked at me, as if he thought me interesting and wanted to know me better. He, a married man who kept a mistress. And like a fool, I thought him handsome. I smiled back and blushed like a schoolgirl.

Shame and horror wash over me. How could I have been so wrong?

The sun! Early this morning the clouds broke, and now the sun shines down on us! The world outside the window gleams white like a fairyland. And the wind blows warmer. The snow will melt soon.

I think if today had been gray yet again, something inside me would have cracked open. For yesterday's revelations continue to shock and anger me.

I know about kissing, and I like it. But other aspects of the relations between men and women . . . well, for me that belongs to the future. Something to wonder about, but not too closely.

Perhaps I considered Emma and Cass much older because they have children. I assumed that the children they have borne began in love. For Emma, that seems to be the case. But for Cass, poor Cass . . . I still feel my skin crawl when I think of her being forced.

It is only the sun warming my shoulders that allows me to push these thoughts away and think instead of this family's deliverance to Canada. It can't come too soon.

Company at last after ten long days. The roads have cleared enough for riders to get through. My brothers came at midday and brought letters and such news as there is from a village wrapped in snow. Can Jeremiah be far behind? I surely hope not.

Tom unloaded baskets of bread, cold chicken, and

cakes from Mama's kitchen. Will handed me a packet of letters.

"Oh, Will, thank you so much. Could you please deliver the ones I've written?"

"I feel like a durned letter carrier," he grumbled. "I'll start charging for delivery." He passed me another letter. "This here's from Jonathan Clark. He hightailed it over to our place before breakfast. How'd you get him so riled up, Lucy? He breathed fire."

"None of your business," I said. My own cheeks flamed.

"Aw, Lucy, tell us," Tom put in. "Will says you got that boy all harnessed and bridled. You don't have to take the whip to him. Just give him a lump of sugar." Tom grinned at me like a wicked, freckled elf.

"And what would you know about such lumps of sugar?"

"I can't say." He grinned again, and I mussed his hair.

"Did you write him back, Luce? If you send him a pile of kisses in your letter, he won't be mad," Will advised. He made loud kissing noises. Tom chimed in, and together they sounded like a wagon with squeaking wheels.

They stayed with Miss Aurelia and me for the midday meal. Later, though my letters burned in my pocket to be read, I felt a tug on my heart as Tom and Will drove away. I didn't know just when I'd see them or the rest of my family again.

"Miss Aurelia, could I read my letters, please?"

"Certainly, Lucy dear. Take all the time you need."

I retreated to my room and curled up on the featherbed. Before I opened a single letter I set them out in front of me like a plate of sweets, choosing which to read first. My family's, for my heart ached with missing them. Then Rebecca's. Finally Jonathan Clark's, for I wasn't sure if his letter would be good news or bad.

19 *January*

Dear Lucinda,

You must be chafing with this storm. I've never known you to sit happily indoors with untrodden snow out the window. And yet, as you tend to our neighbor, I'm sure you put other needs ahead of your own. I am proud, daughter, for your heart is large.

Perhaps I might remind you of the good side of such a storm. Let yourself think of the natural world—how the brown bears curl deep in their winter dens and rest. All God's creatures need such times of rest, as it girds them for the coming spring and for whatever journeys the warming weather will bring.

So accept this respite as a gift for those birds and beasts whose travels are long and whose endurance might be nearing its end. For once the snow melts, the world will wake again with all its cares.

Your brothers and I have used our time well. We mend harness and polish brasses by the fire. Your mother cooks and bakes, as if we need twice the feeding with the storm. But perhaps this is just as well, for she can send some of her cooking to you to lighten your burden of chores.

You are in our thoughts daily, but never as much as in the evenings, when we gather around the hearth. Your mother and I take our turns reading aloud to the younger ones, but we miss your voice and the dramatic way you bring the simple words to life.

We are just now reading some poems of Sir Walter Scott, and young Thomas has determined to memorize "The Lady of the Lake." I guess that means he shall become a gentleman as well as a farmer, for in spite of William's teasing, he labors hard over the pages.

Your mother and I are well pleased with you and with Thomas, our family scholars. I would not be surprised to find that he practices his stanzas out in the barn while he tends to the beasts, both wild and tame. What do you suppose the horses make of all this reciting?

Your loving
Father

22 *January*

My dearest Lucy,

Your papa has stolen all my news. For when snow blankets the earth for days on end, news grows scarce indeed. Mostly we must find ways to entertain ourselves.

I have been teaching Miranda to use the needle. She often pricks her finger, but I've started her on dark cloth, so no spots will show. Do you recall the first sampler you stitched? I brought it out to show your sister so she'd understand that you too were imperfect with your stitches when you were small. But with your sister I have hit upon a lovely idea. Instead of expecting her to make tiny stitches, I have given her small patches of cloth left from this or that project of mine. She is sewing on a crazy quilt for her doll and there is no exact pattern or line required.

Will says I spoil her. Do you think I grow lax with my youngest? Or is this a good notion?

I also felt myself quite clever when I suggested that if Miranda truly wanted to help with hurt or wounded animals, she might someday have to stitch up a cut or gash, so it might be wise to practice first on cloth. Her work grew neater almost right away.

Mostly, however, she trudges to the barn with Thomas, brushes the cat's fur, tells stories to the doe, and tries to encourage the three birds to become friends. Imagine that, Lucy—a duck, a cardinal, and a lopsided hen. Your sister has a mind of her own. But then, as I recall, so did you at her age.

I think this heavy weather is hardest on William. He has grown accustomed to travel and seems to have difficulty staying about the house and farm. He paces and stares out the window. He goes out to fetch wood without our asking and stays out for a long time. At the first break in the weather we'll send him to you with our letters and give him a chance to spread his wings. For, like Miranda's charges and other wild birds, I believe your brother William is meant to fly. Papa says he will settle down and become a farmer, but I'm not so sure.

Oh, Lucy. I rattle on like an old woman. I miss you severely. Having a grown daughter is such a wonder, for I can talk to you as a friend. When you're gone, I feel the lack of women's company. While you are much needed where you are, I do count the days until you are returned to us, and in particular to me.

*Your loving
Mother*

Dear Lucy,

Mama's writing for me again. Doesn't she write pretty? She makes me practice letters every day so that I'll write pretty, too. I'm trying. I can write my name really pretty now. But it's a lot of work. Miranda has seven letters. Lucy is easier and so is Will and so is Tom.

My fingers get tired from writing and from sewing. When the needle pokes my finger it hurts. I try not to cry. Crying is for babies. I want to be big like you and the boys.

Reddie does well. He likes to sing to Queen Victoria, our deer. She is almost healed. Tom says that when Reddie's wing grows strong we'll have to set him free. I don't like that. We don't have to send Hamlet or Ophelia away, so why Reddie? Tom says it's because he's wild.

Fine. I'll make him tame. I'll make Queen Victoria tame, too. I want to send Brutus away. He's a bad cat. He keeps bothering all the birds.

Hamlet and Ophelia are big. They peck at Brutus's nose if he gets close. Poor little Reddie can't do that. I wish we had a harness small enough for a cat. I would tie Brutus to the hitching post. Maybe you can help me make one. Come home soon. I love you.

Miranda

Dear Lucinda,

What a storm! Good thing the Clarks had their party last week instead of this. With all this snow, nobody could have come.

Lucy, what happened at the party? One minute you were spinning wild tales about the migrations of birds; the next time I looked over, you and Jeremiah Strong had disappeared. You were gone a long time, Lucy. Jonathan stomped out to find you and came back furious. Then you went off to Widow Mercer's house.

What an amazing night. Everybody gossiped and speculated—more than usual, if that's possible. Mrs. Clark looked especially cross. When you and your brothers created all that excitement, she was suddenly reduced to fetching baskets. It did my heart good to see her put in her place for once. But beware—I suspect she holds grudges. She may try to come between you and her son. Although he created some ruckus of his own . . .

Jonathan danced every reel with that annoying flirt, Eleanora Cummings, but I bet he stepped on her toes more than once, he was so stirred up. Lucy, what's going on? What happened out there? What did you say to get Jonathan so riled up? Are you in love with Jeremiah Strong now? Or Jonathan Clark? Or both?

You must, must write and tell me everything. Otherwise I'll make up stories in my mind. Oh, and I've had another idea. Remember two Sundays ago in church? We wanted to do another prank. Well, I've thought of one. It's wonderfully wicked. But I won't tell you until you share your news. So there.

Give my best to Widow Mercer. I've written this and will pass it to Nathaniel later today when he comes to take me for a sleigh ride. He'll give it to your brother for you. Wish me luck with Nathaniel, Lucy. The dancing at the party was wonderful, and I think he's about to speak to my father. I hope the widow heals quickly, for her own sake, of course, but mostly so I can see you again soon.

Your friend,
Rebecca

18 *January*

Dear Lucinda,

I have waited a full week for your reply but have received none. Does that mean you don't care for me anymore?

I hope some other reason, such as this terrible snowstorm, keeps your letter from my hands. Pa and I have had to work hard to keep the stock fed and the logs hauled so Ma can keep the house warm and the meals cooked. I worry about you, caring for the widow all by yourself. First fine day, I'll be coming by to visit you.

I've got to see you, Lucinda. All this worry keeps me awake at night, and I can't help but remember the sight of you and that Quaker kissing by the fire. You stuck a knife right into my heart that night, and every time I remember, the knife goes deeper.

Please, dear Lucy. Write back and say you still care for me. Say it was all a mistake and you're sorry. I promise I'll forgive you. Or, if you don't still care about me, at least let me know, for we've been friends a long time, and this is no way to treat an old friend.

I wait for your letter!
Jonathan

I can't sleep. My feelings churn around inside me so hard that if I were a pail of cream, I'd have long ago turned to butter. First I get wonderful letters from Mama and Papa and even dear little Miranda. The home letters make me so lonesome I have to bite back the tears. Rebecca's words cheer me, though, and I'll hold on to her letter for strength, for surely I'll need it to write to Jonathan.

What can I say to him? He promises to forgive me, but what if I don't want to be forgiven? What if his forgiveness doesn't even matter to me? What kind of girl does that make me? If I really loved him, I'd feel guilty.

Or else angry. Rebecca said he danced every single dance with Eleanora Cummings. If I loved him, that would make me furious, but it only tugs a little. If anything hurts, it's just my pride.

Still, I wonder. So much is happening, and so quickly. I thought I loved Jonathan, but now my heart turns toward Jeremiah. Can I trust these treacherous emotions? And would I be a coward to tell Jonathan of my feelings in a letter instead of in person?

I must be cautious, but I don't quite know how. Perhaps a good night's sleep will clear my mind.

I stayed up all night, unable to sleep. I went downstairs and stared into the hearth, looking for answers in the flames.

Miss Aurelia caught me, worse luck.

"Lucinda? What's the matter? You weren't yourself all afternoon, and now you've not slept."

"Oh, Miss Aurelia . . ." I didn't really know her well enough to tell her, but I needed to tell somebody. "It's so confusing."

She looked out the window. "Morning's not far off. Shall I brew some coffee?"

I nodded and watched her make the coffee. It smelled wonderful. She poured me a cup. I added lots of fresh cream and a little sugar and sipped, tasting warmth and comfort.

"Well?"

"I got a letter. Two letters, actually. From Jonathan Clark. Oh, Miss Aurelia, romance is so hard."

"Yes. If my old mind can stretch back, I seem to recall stormy days and sunny ones. Are you sure you want to talk? I'm not one for intruding. Can't stand when people mess about in my business, so I try to stay out of theirs."

Did that mean she didn't want to hear my troubles? Or just that she wouldn't pry? "I don't want to bother you, but . . ."

"But I'm here. I'm the best you'll get just now." She smiled.

"It all started at the Clarks' party," I began. I unrolled the whole thing, tangles and all, like so many lengths of ribbon. She just sat and listened.

"What do I do, Miss Aurelia? I like Jeremiah. But I used to like Jonathan. Maybe I still do. But I can't tell him about the Railroad."

"That's the one clear spot in this muddle," she said. "I'm not sure about the Clark family's loyalties. Especially that mother of his."

"So what will I do?"

"Let's think for a moment." She studied me this way and that, as if I were a horse she wanted to buy. "You have two feet, don't you, Lucy?"

"Yes. Of course I do."

"Stand up, then, girl."

I did but wondered why.

"Just as I thought. You can stand all by yourself. Seems to me, until you make up your mind otherwise, you'll do fine."

"Do fine?" What did she mean?

"You can stand on your own feet, Lucy. You don't need to lean on any man. You're independent, from what I've seen. Like most women, you don't know your own strength."

Her words took me by surprise. "Miss Aurelia! Do you really think women are strong?"

"Not all, but most are. Look at the women you know, dear. Which of them hasn't suffered pain or loss with great courage? Which hasn't borne a handful of children, lost one or two, been forced to make difficult choices? And yet they work as hard or harder than their men."

I thought about it. Mama, my grandmothers, the women in the village—they worked from morning till night, every day of the week. They worked pregnant and sick in every season. And Emma and Cass, fleeing north in the dead of winter. If they weren't strong, who was?

"In the short term you'll need an answer for young Mr. Clark," she continued. "Perhaps you could plead overwork—tell him you need time to sort out your feelings."

"That's true," I said. "I am busy, and very confused."

She nodded. "But you might think hard before you decide anything serious. How long have you worked with the fugitives?"

"I've been helping for four years. Mama and Papa began the work after Papa saw an abolitionist newspaper and heard some speeches. They read books and articles and talked with the Quakers in Salem. Jeremiah's uncle helped us set up a station."

"Lucinda, are these abolitionist beliefs yours, or do they simply belong to your parents?"

I took my time answering. In truth, my beliefs had begun as echoes of my parents' beliefs.

"They're mine," I said at last. "I've heard terrible stories. Whips, brands, chopped-off fingers and toes. And especially now, after what Emma told us about Cass . . . Slavery is wrong." I looked into Miss Aurelia's eyes. "That *is* my belief."

"I don't doubt you, dear. Just wished to provoke your thoughts. But how will you live your life? What will you do about the Railroad if you marry a man who doesn't share your beliefs?"

My breath caught. I'd always assumed I could convince Jonathan of whatever I wanted. That he'd love me enough to join in my work. But would he? What would I do if he didn't? Could I still care about him then? Did I even want to?

I studied Miss Aurelia's lean, oval face, the soft brown curls that escaped her thick bun. For a woman who didn't like to interfere, she had just turned my life upside down.

SUNDAY, JANUARY 26, 1851

Dear Lord, You held out Your hand to us today when we needed You desperately. Please, deliver these people from danger as fast as You can. We came so close this afternoon. . . .

I was dozing by the fire when I heard horses in the distance. At first I assumed it was Will and Tom, coming to help or visit. I shook myself awake. What if it wasn't my brothers?

I hurried to the kitchen. "Miss Aurelia. Horses."

"I'll go up to the attic and warn everybody. You check for signs of our visitors."

"But you're supposed to be sick in bed!"

"I will be," she said. "Hurry. See to the kitchen."

I walked around. The table looked tidy enough, but there were too many plates out for just the two of us. I set some in the cupboard. My heart beat double time and my cheeks flushed. I scanned the room. What else could give us away?

"Lucy! Lucy!"

I ran for the door and flung it open. "Tom?"

"Oh, Lucy. Bad news. Catchers coming, soon. They're at our house now, snooping everywhere. I was in the barn helping Papa when they came. They didn't see me. Papa sent me to warn you."

"How many?"

"Five men, four dogs. Lucy, what can we do?"

I thought for a minute. "Chores," I said. "Rub the sweat from your horse with straw. Then haul water and bring in firewood. Pretend you've been here an hour. I'll start corn bread. But first help me look around the house. What have I missed?"

I hurried to the stairs and called up a warning to Miss Aurelia and our hidden visitors.

Tom came in and studied the house. "What's that pile? Sewing? Looks like children's clothes."

"Where can I put it?" I heard panic in my voice and took a deep breath. If the catchers or their dogs caught a sound or a scent of fear, they'd find us out for sure. My head pounded.

"Hide them in the wash basket, Lucy. Under something."

"Good idea. Stable your horse and bring wood now, and water."

Tom ran outside. I hid the clothing, then tied a big apron on and threw together cornmeal, bacon grease, some milk, and eggs.

In a blink Tom returned with a full bucket. "Lucy, I'm worried about them dogs."

"What?"

"You got lots of people here. You made lots of trips up to the attic. The dogs will smell something."

I thought quickly. At home Mama hung smoked hams and bacon in the root cellar to confuse any dogs who might come. I set out some bacon, to add smells to the kitchen, but what about the door to the attic? Whoever heard of putting ham upstairs?

"Oh, Tom! The dogs will surely catch a scent in that back bedroom. What stinks enough to confuse them?"

He chewed his bottom lip. "I don't know, Lucy. Give me a minute."

Fists hammered at the door. "We don't have a minute, Tom. Get upstairs and think of something, quick."

The racket grew louder. Tom raced for the stairs.

I wiped my sweaty hands on my apron and headed for the door. "Who's there?"

"Beggin' your pardon, miss, but we got business with you."

"I . . . I don't know your voice. Who is it, please?"

"That you, Lucinda Spencer? It's me, Levi Bowen. I been deputized by the magistrate. We got us a Southern boy here, looking for lost property."

Levi Bowen, a man from Limaville. A lazy good-for-nothing, according to Papa, but I knew him. I couldn't keep the door barred any longer. I trembled as I opened it.

"Mr. Bowen. How may I help you?"

"We got to search the place," he said. "This fella had a passel of slaves run off. We're checking every house in the village. We caught the man, but the women and children got away."

"I've been so busy tending Widow Mercer, I've hardly seen my own shadow," I said. "But come in if you must."

"Thank you. This here's Clayton Roberts, the owner of the runaways. Him and some boys."

I forced a look of casual curiosity onto my face as I nodded to Clayton Roberts. Here, close up, I faced the evil man who had mistreated Cass. Ruth and Mesha's natural father. He smiled at me. I balled my hands into fists behind my back and felt my nails dig into my palms.

"You've had measles, then?" I asked. "The widow's still feverish." I hoped Miss Aurelia had sipped some whiskey so that her face would be red and hot. And what was keeping Tom?

The slave owner turned to his men. "You boys go out and check the barn and outbuildings. Take three of the dogs with you. I'll check the inside."

Only one dog inside—that was good. But his nose would surely find us out. *Tom, please! Think of something,* I prayed silently.

"If the widow's upstairs, I could look down here," Levi Bowen offered. "Don't suppose I'd catch no measles from that far."

Good-for-nothing coward. Papa was right.

Something thumped above our heads.

"Dad blast it!"

It was Tom at last. Hallelujah!

"Thomas Spencer, what have you done now?" I ran for the stairs, yanked up my skirts, and took the steps two at a time. I stood in the doorway of the back bedroom, the one with the secret door.

"Aw, Lucy, this ain't my job. You shouldn't of made me do it."

"I've never seen such a mess!" Tom had dumped ashes from the fireplace all across the center of the room. As I hollered he marched around and spread them further.

I stood in the doorway and coughed at the smoky smell. "I'll bring you a bucket and rags," I said. "You don't leave this room until the floor shines. Then you'll have a bath."

"Naw, not a bath, too! You'll make me into a girl!"

I heard chuckles behind me, so I knew we had an audience. I turned. "If you will forgive me," I began, "I'm afraid I lost my temper. My brother was in too big a hurry again. I can show you about the house. Widow Mercer's room is right here. She was resting, but I doubt she slept through all that commotion."

I scowled at Tom for good measure. He stuck out his tongue.

The slave owner chuckled again. He smiled his most charming smile and let me pass. I pointed him toward Miss Aurelia, then stomped down the stairs.

The men took a long while to search the house and barn. After I got Tom his rags and pail, I stayed in the kitchen and mixed up the corn bread. I paced in front of the stove while it baked.

"Smells mighty good, Lucy," Tom called. "Can I have a piece?"

"You got that floor clean yet?"

He groaned. "You're starving me, Luce."

At last the men finished. "Would you take some warm corn bread along?" I asked. "It's a bitter afternoon."

"Thank you, Miss Spencer," Clayton Roberts said. He shook my hand and held it for a minute. I wanted to yank it away, but I was afraid to make him suspicious. I gritted my teeth and grinned.

"Sorry if we caused a sweet young lady like you any inconvenience." He flashed his blue eyes in my direction in a look that bothered me. Did he suspect something? Want something from me? I felt as if he was searching my face, touching me with his eyes. Inwardly I cringed.

"Not at all," I said. "These are difficult times." If they only knew how difficult! I cut the corn bread into large pieces and passed one to each man. Drat, I wished I'd put pepper in the batter, or too much salt.

I stood beside the door and watched until the men mounted their horses and disappeared down the road.

"Waste of good corn bread," Tom said, coming up beside me. He snitched a piece and stuffed it into his mouth with sooty fingers.

"Wait till Mama catches sight of you," I said. "She'll dunk you in the tub for a week."

"It was worth it, Lucy," he said. "That rotten slaver and his dirty dog never even stuck their noses in that room. I made a real good mess." His eyes sparkled with mischief.

"You did." I ruffled his hair. "I'm proud of you. Now we've got serious scrubbing to do."

But as I knelt next to Tom and scrubbed at the sooty stains, I couldn't imagine a soap strong enough to wash away the meanness and evil of Clayton Roberts, a man who could sell off his own children. For all his brilliant blue eyes, he had the soul of a snake. He'd made me so mad, I'd probably wear through a whole layer of Miss Aurelia's wood floor.

As I sit here and remember, I feel an itch in the palms of my hands. An un-Christian urge, surely, but if I ever see that Clayton Roberts again, I'll have to fight the temptation to pound his face into the rich brown mud of the free state of Ohio.

MONDAY, JANUARY 27, 1851

Melting, melting, and more melting. The sun has showed its face to us for five days in a row and melted the snow into gray slush. But I would give up the sunshine in a minute if it meant no more visits like the one yesterday. All day today, as I scrubbed dirty clothing and hauled it up to the attic to dry, I jumped at shadows and startled at small sounds.

Jeremiah, where are you? Why do you take so long? When will this all be over?

TUESDAY, JANUARY 28, 1851

I now count twelve days since Jeremiah left his letter for me in the door. Waiting is the hardest thing in the world. I hate it!

So I wrote my duty letter to Jonathan Clark, as Miss Aurelia suggested. It was short but not too mean, I hope.

WEDNESDAY, JANUARY 29, 1851

Wretched day all around. The baby fussed, the milk went sour from sitting in the sun too long, and Jeremiah still didn't come. Has he dropped from the face of the earth?

THURSDAY, JANUARY 30, 1851

Fourteen days now that Jeremiah has been gone. Is he truly in danger? Or is he just having a grand adventure and forgetting about those of us who wait back home? I try to keep faith that Jeremiah will return, and soon. I read his letter every night before I go to bed, but still I wonder.

FRIDAY, JANUARY 31, 1851
VERY EARLY

Hallelujah! Jeremiah has returned. I heard pebbles on my window not an hour ago, and when I went to the door he was standing on the porch. He opened his arms, and I ran to him and held on until my feet began to freeze.

"Lucinda, how I have missed thee."

"Jeremiah, it's been more than two weeks! Whatever happened?"

"We rescued Abraham. I carried him to Cleveland in my sleigh. The journey was long and harsh, but the roads were mostly empty. The most difficult part was returning here, for the sun has turned the road into a swamp."

"Cleveland! No wonder it took so long! But you're back. I'm so glad."

"Back, but not for long. We must remove the family from this house. Every day thy risk of being found out grows more severe."

"Oh, Jeremiah, he came here. That slave owner and some men. They searched the house and barns. Tom warned us, but if he hadn't . . . I hate to think . . ."

"All the more reason to carry them north right away. I've not been home yet. I stopped at thy house before coming here. William will come with his wagon when darkness falls tonight. I will join him on the edge of town. If thee and Sister Mercer can make the visitors ready to travel . . ."

"We can." I felt suddenly shy. "I've written you a letter. You'll find it when you reach home."

"I've written to thee as well. Not a letter exactly, but notes of the journey. I have written this for thy eyes only, without the usual cautions, for I intended to place it in thy hands directly. But for thy sake I did not use thy name. I addressed thee as 'dear friend.' Know this, Lucinda: I wrote these words for thee and thee only."

"You wrote freely? That's dangerous for you. If caught . . ."

"The entire trip was dangerous. But I had to write thee honestly. If caught, I'd have found a way to burn the pages."

He kissed me, and we held each other for a long time. Then he was gone, hoofbeats receding in the distance. I stayed on the porch, warmed by the kisses, until I could no longer hear him. I hurried inside to stir up the fire and read the packet he had thrust into my hands.

My fingers shake, for the news is both glorious and difficult.

17 January

I have raced against the snow this day. I began before first light with wagon wheels but soon traded them for sleigh runners. The road to Canton grew ever whiter, but I have good horses and we made a fine day's journey, halfway at the least. I traveled well enough, for though the snow fell and winds blew, my heart was warm with thoughts of thee.

18 January

Canton at last after an arduous journey. The snow alone would have been bad, but the winds blew up great drifts and left nearly bare patches of ground, which caught the runners. I had to always watch the road and sometimes steer across fields instead.

Sorry news waited in Canton. Friend Eli Whitman stands accused and convicted of violating the Fugitive Slave Act. Because he is a Friend and a peaceable man of God, he will not be sent to jail, but the magistrate has levied the maximum fine, one thousand dollars. We are to pass the word to all Friends' meetings and ask for support—otherwise he and his family shall lose their farm. Pray for our effort, dear friend. I fear this is just the start. And guard thyself and thy charges well. My heart is heavy with worry for Friend Whitman and for thee.

19 *January*

No silent and prayerful meeting for this Friend this First Day. Under cover of night and the storm, three of us from Salem—supposed men of peace—broke into the jail and removed Abraham. My conscience scolds, for we had to restrain the deputy who sat on duty, but we did not inflict violence upon him. Rather, we sneaked up behind, covered his eyes and mouth, and tied him to his chair.

Could I have hurt the man to save Abraham? I don't know. The Lord requires of us that we love even our enemies. We placed him, chair and all, closer to the fire, and we added extra logs before we left so that he would not freeze before morning. I hope he will be all right, but we dared not linger to make sure, for the road and Cleveland awaited.

Wish me Godspeed, for thy mission and mine are but two wheels of the same cart.

20 *January*

We rest this day in a barn outside of Randolph. So near to thee, I am sorely tempted to sneak away and visit, but I must not. Abraham is in good spirits now that he has got over the shock of our rescue and the cold weather. He shivers visibly, although we have been well provided with clothing, quilts, and straw to keep the worst of the wind from him. He said to me, "One day you gonna make a journey to my old Carolina. Feel the hot sun on your back. Then you know why I chill."

My fellow conspirators have taken their leave, and Abraham and I alone shall travel north. It will be a long journey in these freezing conditions, but Abraham says freedom will warm his heart and his family once they are reunited. I need no trip to

Carolina to understand that sort of warmth, for when I think of thee, the storm is but a snow shower.

21 January

On to Hudson. At first light the town still slept under a coverlet of snow. Beautiful. I wished for thee at my side to see it. Someday, perhaps. We made a long night journey, and the wind grows harsh as we settle in the attic of a trusted soul. I pray the wind will blow these gray clouds away, for the storm has hovered too long. Warm food and a day's rest is a gift beyond measure.

22 January

Another night of travel has brought us to Bedford. Under other circumstances I might grow tired or cold, but my purpose is strong. Each day, as we draw closer to the lake, Abraham's face loses a bit of its worry. To my eyes, he grows younger every mile. He is not nearly so old a man as I first thought.

I remind him that once he is well and safely hidden, we shall have to make another such trip with his family. He says he'll pray for the sun to shine on their passage and will we please wrap them in many quilts to stay warm.

I would like to wrap thee in my arms—that is my notion of staying warm. Is that too forward of me, dear friend? I hope not, for I have fond memories of thy kiss. Have I brought a blush to thy cheek? I hope so.

23 January

Cleveland at last. And the sun shines upon us—God's blessing, I am convinced. This night we rest in the stable outside the town, but we will search out a safer, warmer place, for Abraham may have a long wait. I suggested to him that he might make the voyage to Canada immediately, but he will not. He intends to wait for his family.

I would do the same, dear friend. I could not cross the lake alone and let such an expanse of rough water come between thee and me. Still, his waiting will bring risks, and he is so close to reaching freedom. I argue this with him, and he replies, "What be freedom without my Emma?" I am ashamed to have brought it up.

24 January

The wharves in Cleveland are watched. There are regular patrols, such as the one that caught Friend Whitman, and worse, there are spies who congregate in taverns along the waterfront. The barbershop we once used is no longer safe. Likewise the rooming house. We shall have to hide Abraham farther from the lake. I am torn. I must stay with this man until he is safely settled, for he trusts me. And yet I long to return to thee. And no, my wish to return is not only selfish, for when I come to thee, I shall also bring Abraham's family to him and all shall be safe sooner. I count the moments.

25 January

Another day fruitlessly searching for a hiding place. We Friends learn patience from the cradle, for we wait upon the

Lord, but my patience wears thin. I am urging Him to action. Where is the haven we seek for Abraham? As the sun shines and the snow melts, activity alongside the docks increases. Our risks grow. Keep us in thy prayers, dear friend, for we sorely need them.

26 January

At last. I attended meeting this First Day morning and prayed devoutly. The Lord led me to a Friend who owns a large warehouse. If Abraham can abide the smell of fish, he will rest safe and I can return to thee. I will travel as fast as my horses can carry me.

27 January

Bedford again, and now I travel during daylight hours, for I travel alone—Abraham waits among the fish barrels. A good thing, too, for the snow melts and the roads are muck. I need every caution as I drive. Tonight I'll change my sleigh runners for wagon wheels, but I fear this will slow the journey. Perhaps we'll get a cold snap and everything will freeze over. Then I could skate home to thee.

28 January

Hudson is not nearly so pretty in mud as it is in snow. Or perhaps my eyes grow impatient. Too many days have passed on the road, and I yearn for home and thee.

29 *January*

I made Ravenna but had to travel well into darkness to do so. One of my wheels broke at midday and I had to put on the spare wheel knee-deep in muddy slush. I am weary, weary, weary of travel and of winter. Only thoughts of thee keep me from hiding away in a barn until the roads dry.

30 *January*

It is midday and I shall write only a little. I will make Atwater tonight or else. Home is close. The horses and I can smell it. Soon, dear friend, soon!

FRIDAY, JANUARY 31, 1851
AFTERNOON

Jeremiah! His news to me was so sweet I stayed up till dawn to savor it. He missed me every bit as much as I missed him! It gladdens my soul that his purpose and mine are the same. For all that he is a Quaker and I am a Presbyterian, we are alike in the ways that matter.

I thought *my* chores were hard—how difficult it was for him. At least I was warm indoors and protected from the worst of the storm.

I don't like that he must make another trip north so soon, but I'll endure it. He journeyed well in spite of the storm and will journey well again. If only I could go instead of Will. Bah! The rules are too strict for girls. But I'll obey, for what choice do I have?

Tomorrow I'll return home to Mama and Papa, to Tom and Miranda and all their wild beasts. Home! The word is as sweet as snow candy on my tongue.

FEBRUARY

I couldn't write last night. Couldn't bear it.

Yesterday was the saddest day. It started so wonderfully, I still have a hard time understanding why it had to go wrong. The only worse thing would have been a return visit from that slave owner. Thank the Lord he didn't come.

Miss Aurelia and I bustled about all day, cooking and packing clothing. The attic hummed with energy. Emma kept calling out, "Glory be!" and we sang as we worked.

Cass didn't sing. I figured she was saving her energy for the trip. We found out different when Will came at darkness with his wagon.

I gave Emma a bottle of paregoric Mama had sent and explained how to dose the littlest children so they'd sleep, not cry and call attention to themselves.

Emma nodded. "We ready. We all wearing two sets of clothes to stay warm. Glory be, Cass, can you believe it? We be real and true free in a few days."

Cass hadn't said much all day. She hadn't changed clothes yet, either. I looked at her and saw a single tear slip down her cheek.

"I can't go," she said. "I lose this baby if I go. You maybe lose your Cass, too. I feeling too poorly. I got to rest."

"Cass, the trip take only three or four days. You got to come."

Cass shook her head.

"We can't go," Emma said. She gripped my hand tight and her voice caught. "Get word to Abraham. Tell him to get across that water and make a place for us. We come as soon as we can."

"No," Cass said. "Could be weeks yet. Go now. Mister Roberts, he be back. Take my babies north. Keep them safe. I come when I can." She turned her face to her pillow.

Emma stood and hugged herself. "Why God doing this?" she demanded. "Why He make me choose, my sister or my man?"

"God didn't do this," I said. "Men did, evil ones." I hated the words I needed to say next, but I said them anyway. "Look, Emma, if Cass knows you and her children are safe, she'll rest better. She'll gain strength for when her baby comes."

"But the catchers . . ."

"Miss Aurelia and I can hide one woman easier than a whole family. I promise, as soon as Cass can travel she and the baby will come to Canada, even if I have to drive them myself."

Emma took a deep breath. Her face took on a hard, stiff expression. I waited, hoping she'd make the wise and safe choice.

Could I decide between Tom and Will? Mama and Papa? Could I ever leave Miranda behind? I felt ashamed yet everlastingly grateful that I didn't have to choose between those I loved.

At last Emma spoke, and my heart thudded with every word.

"Ben, Shad, gals, get loaded now. We going north to Daddy." She turned to me and tried to smile, but her face had gone gray.

The goodbyes were terrible. Emma sat and hugged Cass. Both women kept their faces blank, holding back hurt, but tears flowed like rain. "You come north soon as that baby get born, Cassie."

"What? Bossing me again, Emmaline? I come soon as I can." Cass gave her sleepy children a long hug and kiss. She passed them over to Emma. "My children in good hands."

"Mama," Ruth cried, "I don't want to go without you." She buried her face in her mother's nightgown.

Cass held the child close. "Ruthie, remember your

naming story. We one family. You be Naomi's people, she be your people." Cass kissed Ruth and placed her hand in Naomi's. "Emma take care of you now. You help with the littler ones. Practice up for this new baby I gonna bring. I love you, Ruthie. Be a good girl."

Miss Aurelia herded the older children toward the steps. Emma kissed Cass once more and moved toward the stairs, a child on each hip. We all dragged out to the barn.

Will had shifted his cargo to one side and lifted the floorboards to expose the hidden compartment in the bottom of his wagon.

Emma took charge. She set the little ones into the wagon and found places for the older ones. Then she turned and hugged me and Miss Aurelia before climbing in herself.

I kissed all the children and tucked blankets around them. Miss Aurelia set a basket of food by Ben's feet. After spending so long with us, they left much too quickly. Within minutes Miss Aurelia and I helped Will shift hay bales back into place over the false bottom of the wagon.

"Drive carefully, William," Miss Aurelia said. "Don't take any chances. If you need more time for safety, take it."

"I'll do my best," he said.

I hugged my brother tight. "God bless you, Will. Godspeed."

My eyes teared up as he clicked to his horses and headed north under a starry sky. I looked for the Big Dipper and the North Star, which pointed their way, until Will had disappeared into the night and all I could hear was the muffled clop of hoofbeats. Only one thought gave me a shred of comfort—Will would be meeting up with Jeremiah at the edge of town—so our friends would be in the best of all possible hands.

Miss Aurelia and I returned to the house. It felt empty as a cornfield in winter. Heartsore, I rearranged the clean pots on Miss Aurelia's stove and turned all the teacups so the handles faced the same way.

"Lucy, don't be sorry they've gone," she cautioned. "We succeeded."

"I know. But I can miss them, can't I? I can worry about Cass. How will she have her baby without Emma?"

"My neighbor, Bessie Smith, is a midwife," Miss Aurelia said. "She'll assist Cass with her labor when the time comes." She took my hand. "But for now, a prayer or two might ease your heart and our friends' journey. Shall we?"

We sat by the fire and bowed our heads in silent supplication for my brother, Emma, all the children, and Cass.

"Amen," she said. "Now sleep. You've earned it. I'll sit with Cass." Her voice sounded just like Mama's no-nonsense voice, and out of habit I obeyed.

1 *February*

Dear Mama,

Bless you for sending Tom with the wagon to fetch me home. As you know by now, illness keeps me with Miss Aurelia longer than we'd expected. My heart aches for you and Papa and the cozy room I share with sweet Miranda, but I have no choice. I cannot leave Miss Aurelia to face possible complications alone. I see my duty here, and I will stay until her health returns and my work is complete.

Mama, pray a lot. Pray for all those whose hearts are sore this day, and for the sick who need God's healing love. Pray for me too, for I am weak and my spirits sink at the hard choice I have made. And please, Mama, spare Tom whenever you can and send him to us. His round, freckled face is the sweetest sight in the world to me, for he reminds me of you and the loving home that awaits when my work is done.

I am sorry to be such a crybaby. I am ashamed as well, for there are those whose hurts cut much deeper than mine. I will rise tomorrow and try to find strength and cheer, but for now my heart brims with sadness.

Lucinda

SUNDAY, FEBRUARY 2, 1851

I want. I want. I want. The list is so long I feel greedy. Here is what I want—

    Cass to get better and have a healthy child

    Will and Jeremiah to deliver Emma and the children to Cleveland

    A boat and safe passage to Canada for them all

    To live in a place where there is no slavery

That is a fine and righteous list. For myself, I count but two wishes—

    For my brother and Jeremiah to return safely

    To go home

I tried to cheer Cass today but failed miserably. She just lies there in bed up in that huge empty attic and stares at the roof. She doesn't cry out loud, but tears leak from her eyes. And she barely eats. How can we improve her spirits?

And mine. For Mama sent Tom with a letter that made me lonelier still.

1 *February*

Dear, sweet Lucy,

The clouds pile ever so high, and the wind grows strong. I fear another storm. I worry that you and Aurelia have enough firewood and food. We pray for your safety every morning and every night. Our house is quiet. No visitors, and only chores to keep us occupied. Your papa sits and whittles legs for a new bench, but he fidgets. I know his thoughts stray to you as well.

Miranda is a bee in a bottle. She buzzes to get out, but it's too cold. Where that child gets her energy, I'll never know. She's made me promise to write down her news next, and I will, but I must tell you how she misses you. I sympathize, being a younger sister. I believed my older sister was a queen, ruler of my world. My universe crumbled when she married and left home for Sandusky and the Firelands.

But I guess this separation may be good for us. You are, after all, a young woman now. We wouldn't clip your wings or keep you fenced in our yard. You will soon be queen of your own domain, a wife and then a mother.

I am such a sentimentalist. With half of my heart I want

to hold you back, to clutch my firstborn chick to my breast. And with the other half I envy your youth and your energy. You will soon step into your own life, and that's tremendously exciting.

Shame on me. See what this gray sky has done to my disposition. I shall become more cheerful and less melancholy right away. I think I'll bake a pie. If Miranda helps, it will keep her out of trouble, for a while at least.

We love you, Lucy. Come home to us soon. I'll put this note into Tom's pocket and send him tomorrow.

Love,
Mama

I can barely read the last words, my eyes have fogged up so. But I feel Mama's care and warmth slip around me like loving arms, comforting me, even from a distance.

It's odd how distance has freed her to put new thoughts to words . . . thoughts about my future. We've talked before about it—she taught me to sew and we filled a wooden chest with sheets and pillowslips for my own home. But this letter refers to a close-up future. Too close. I'm not nearly ready to leave my family.

I need to stop sniffling and mucking about. I'll push the serious thoughts aside and read Miranda's note, for surely that will cheer me up.

Dear Lucy,
    Bad news.
    Reddie flew away today.

I cried. I wanted to keep him in his box.

Tom says I shouldn't mind so. He says God didn't make birds for us to shut in boxes. He says they should be free.

I still don't like it. And I don't like it that you're gone. How long do measles take? You belong with us and not Widow Mercer.

Mama says you'll come back soon. She says Reddie might come back. He might bring a lady bird and start a nest near our house. I hope so. And I want you to come home right away. Right away.

Love,
Miranda

Not you too, Miri! Now I'm a real mess, missing everybody—even Tom, whom I've just seen. I'll get up and splash cool water from the basin onto my face. How can I become a grown person if I act like such a child? And how can I feel so sorry for myself when Cass lies upstairs, more alone than I can even imagine?

TUESDAY, FEBRUARY 4, 1851

Perhaps it was loneliness that did it. Or else God answered some of my prayers. Whatever the reason, I'm truly grateful.

In spite of a new snowstorm, Cass and I had a lovely afternoon together. Surprising, actually, because we started off blubbering.

I carried her a plate of fresh hot corn bread, ham, and turnips. She pushed the plate aside.

"You need to eat, Cass. I know you feel terrible, but

think about the baby. You need to eat so the baby can get strong."

She frowned at me. "What you know about terrible?"

I sighed. "I don't, really. It's just that I haven't been away from home before. I feel bad and miss my family, even though they're just a little distance from here. I shouldn't be homesick. Your family's much farther and you've left home for good." I reached up and rubbed at my eyes. I surely didn't want to cry.

She took my hand and sniffed. "You right about that. I did leave home *for good*. Even alone, I feel *good* not to have that master bother me. But my babies . . . I wonder where they be."

Next thing I knew we were hugging each other and crying like babies ourselves. It was then the idea came to me. "Wait! I'll show you where your children are. I bet Miss Aurelia has a map. You eat your dinner, I'll eat mine, and afterward we'll look at the map."

Well, I was so excited I could barely eat. Miss Aurelia produced a map of Ohio, and I got out Jeremiah's letters from his snowy trip so I'd be able to guess what towns he and Will might stop in. I don't know how many times we traced the route from Atwater to Cleveland and then across Lake Erie to Canada, but I know it was enough, for Cass blessed me with a smile. Hallelujah!

WEDNESDAY, FEBRUARY 5, 1851

Will and Jeremiah must have reached Cleveland by now. I'm sure they'll stay put until they see the boat leave the dock, so I'll not calculate or guess about their return, for I'll be disappointed again. But I hope it's soon.

Meanwhile, Cass keeps me busy. I wish I could take credit for another good idea, but this one belongs to her.

We looked at the map again this morning. She pointed at a town. "What this place, Lucy? I not sure I remember."

"That's Hudson. Halfway to Cleveland."

"How you know for sure?"

"It says so, right on the map. That word, there." I pointed. "Hudson."

"How you learn about words, Lucy?"

"Mama taught me some. Mostly I learned at school. You didn't get to go, did you?"

She shook her head.

I know most slaves can't read. Some older folks can, and a few have masters who actually teach them to read the Bible. But way back before I was born, the politicians in most Southern states passed laws that forbid anyone to teach slaves to read.

"Do it be hard? Words?"

"Not really. It takes some time, but anyone can learn it. Even my sister, and she's only five."

"How about me? What I got but time?"

"You mean it? You want to learn to read? You want me to teach you?" I wanted to jump up and down, swing Cass in a do-si-do. "We'll start right away."

I took to teaching as though I'd been born in a schoolroom. We started with Cass's name and her children's and sped through half the alphabet before she grew tired and needed a nap. Cass is as thirsty for learning as a cornfield in a drought.

I rushed downstairs to share the good news with Miss Aurelia. She offered to do all the inside chores, saying that if I can keep Cass happy, that's the most important job of all. Two days ago I would have complained that nobody could keep Cass happy. Now I can barely sit still till she wakes up.

THURSDAY, FEBRUARY 6, 1851

Cass is really funny.

"I like the snaky ones," she said this morning as I taught her the alphabet. "Sssss!"

She wrote her name in my journal, proud as can be.

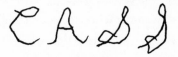

Miss Aurelia gave us paper, and I've written out each letter and a picture that shows the sound it makes. Cass helped with the pictures, for I can't draw worth a peach pit. But between us we have the alphabet done, large and small letters. Tomorrow we'll list the names of her whole family, for Cass works her hardest if the learning tickles her or connects to something important.

Hunger is amazing. Cass has learned more in three days than Miranda learned in three months. Being grown probably helps, but wanting something for so long and then having a chance at it—well, it's all I can do to get her to take her naps. She'd sit and trace letters from dawn until twilight if we let her. But for the baby's sake she needs to rest. Even I know that much.

SATURDAY, FEBRUARY 8, 1851

I'm writing letters to the family and notes in my journal while Cass practices her letters and short words. She asked if she could write something more in my book and so she did. I only helped with the spelling.

CASS WILL MAKE FREE!

8 *February*

Dear Miranda,

Another big storm. Have you made snow angels yet? I bet you have. Next time you go outside, please make an extra one for me.

I have thought about your friend the redbird. Tom is right, Miri dear. Birds are meant to fly. Always.

When it gets warmer, you and I will put snips of Mama's yarn outside so that if Reddie flies by to visit, he and his lady bird will see the yarn and make a nest with it. Won't it be fun to watch them lay eggs and hatch them? I can't wait.

Until then, be a good girl and help Mama.

I love you,
Lucy

8 *February*

Dear Mama and Papa,

I feel so much better now. Even the storm didn't make me feel gray, for it came and went quickly, leaving lovely white fields in place of that dreary mud. Will should be home from his traveling soon, and this heartens me, as it must hearten you. So I write these brief notes for him to carry.

Pray for us all that this winter will pass quickly into spring.

Your loving daughter,
Lucinda

8 *February*

Dear Rebecca,

I will stay with Miss Aurelia a while longer, for illness can be unpredictable. I do miss you, but I keep myself as busy as I can and the time flows by. Not a rushing stream, you understand, but a gently meandering creek. When spring comes we shall have to steal at least a week together, for between your news and mine, a day or two would never be enough.

You have read by now of my romantic quandaries. My

heart leans toward Jeremiah Strong. He is a good man and we share many interests. Doesn't that sound noble? Truth is, he kisses so sweetly it makes me greedy for more. Wicked!

Poor Jonathan Clark. I like him—but as a friend. Now that I have come to care for Jeremiah, I know that mere friendship is not enough. I still struggle for a way to tell Jonathan that is honest and considerate. Is this possible? I hope so.

How is Nathaniel? Has he spoken to your father? Write me everything, for with the winter and the isolation of the widow's illness, my only news comes in letters.

And what prank have you invented? I have told you my secrets. You must now share your mischief with me. Write soon.

Best of luck with Nathaniel,
Lucinda

SUNDAY, FEBRUARY 9, 1851

Am I a dolt? When will I ever learn to look beyond the obvious?

Thick clouds filled the sky today. While Cass napped, I studied them, trying to gauge whether they carried a light storm or a blizzard. I don't like the notion of Will and Jeremiah in bad weather.

"Lucinda, you're a million miles away," Miss Aurelia said.

"I am," I admitted. "Do you have work for me? I've caught up with my letters and journal writing, and Cass will sleep awhile."

"Well, a child will arrive one of these days," she said.

"You might stitch up some clothing. I've scraps in a trunk upstairs."

"All right. How long do you suppose until she has the baby? Emma said a couple of months, but that was weeks ago."

Not that I wish it to come right away. If anything, I worry about the baby's coming. Mama's last birthing has left me fearful.

"Have you warned the midwife, Mrs. Smith? We might need her soon." I tried to keep the worry out of my voice.

Miss Aurelia smiled and spoke calmly. "I've sent a message. Her husband, Jonas, helps me at times, and I've spoken with him. We'll talk to Cass after your brother returns with good news of her family."

I nodded and looked out into the snowy afternoon. Where were they? Were they near Atwater, or had they been delayed in Cleveland? Bah! My wondering wasn't about to hurry the wagons, so I went to fetch the cloth— flannel, muslin, calico, and trimmings.

Miss Aurelia provided me with scissors, a needle, and thread, and I cleared off the kitchen table and set to work. I had done this before with Mama, when Miranda was expected, and again for the child Mama lost last spring.

I started with the largest lengths of flannel and cut them into swaddling blankets.

Miss Aurelia sat across the room by the fire, and I heard the scratch of pencil on paper as I threaded my needle.

"What are you doing?" I asked. "Sketching? Can you draw?"

"Well enough," she said.

"Can I see?"

"Not yet. I'll finish this, then you tell me what you think. I make my living with my pictures, you know."

"By drawing? Did you paint all the pictures on the walls here? I never saw a house with so many."

"Most of them are mine, yes." She smiled.

I stared over her head at a painting of a field of wildflowers in soft yellows and pinks. I could almost smell the fragrance of spring. "How do you make a living from drawing?"

She smiled again and kept her eyes on her work as she spoke. "I'm not exactly a farmer, Lucy. My drawings and stories bring me a good portion of my income."

"You sell drawings and stories? Where?"

"Magazines. Newspapers. They like that I can draw as well as write, so they don't have to find a separate artist."

I shook my head, confused. "You said you weren't a farmer. But I've seen your fields. You grow corn, hay, wheat, barley."

"Lucy, for a perceptive girl, you've missed a bit. Did you never wonder how a widow woman might manage to plow and harvest? If you want pure truth, I'm not even a widow."

I poked my thumb with the point of my needle. "Ouch!" I stuck the thumb in my mouth and sucked it for a minute.

Miss Aurelia laughed. "From the look on your face, we'll need a long talk. Give me a moment to brew some tea. I'll check Cass, then you and I will share secrets. No doubt you'll have three swaddling blankets finished by the time I've answered your questions."

While she bustled with the kettle and went upstairs, I took a closer look at the pictures in the kitchen. Then I cut out more blankets. If we had an afternoon of secrets ahead, I didn't want to cause any distraction. I'd just sit and stitch, and maybe sew some of Miss Aurelia's words into the seams, for strength and for humor. I wanted to be ready for whatever secrets she was willing to share, woman to woman. In truth, I couldn't wait.

MONDAY, FEBRUARY 10, 1851

I am still amazed. Miss Aurelia told me she'd had an unconventional life. What a puny word for such choices!

Her story started simply enough. Her family had come here, to Ohio's Western Reserve, from Connecticut at the start of the century, same as mine had. They'd settled, cleared land, and established farms. Her father had been successful, his brother had not, so her family took charge of his farm too and the brother moved on.

"You know where Jonas and Bessie Smith live?" she asked. "My parents built that cabin. I lease the farm to the Smiths and this farm's fields as well."

That explained the cultivated fields. I turned the corner of the blanket I was hemming and folded down the third long side. Much of this history was as familiar to me as corn bread. I wanted to get on to the secrets.

Miss Aurelia continued. "Father traded timber for finished furniture. He trapped game and sold the pelts at good prices. I met Andrew Mercer through Father's fur trading.

"First, I should tell you that I was my parents' only child. Mother had miscarriage after miscarriage. I was born six years after their marriage, and they'd nearly given up hope of a child by then. So they indulged me. Gave me my way.

"Andrew trapped and worked with Father. When I set my eye on him, Father and Mother agreed, of course. They determined to give my uncle's farm to us. This farm. Father and Andrew began building this house, and while it went up, Father hired a furniture maker from Pittsburgh to come and build the tables and chairs and beds, all crafted from our own fine hardwood trees. They planned a grand and glorious house for their only daughter."

Miss Aurelia spoke lightly, as if making fun. But I'd found the house grand and glorious from the moment I walked in the door.

"I should have paid more attention to the people around me than to the poster beds and canopies," she said. "Mother grew ill. Female troubles, probably related to all those lost children. And she wouldn't spoil my happiness with complaints.

"When we realized she was seriously ill, Andrew and I married quickly, so she could see her daughter's future assured before she died. How foolish—I, an indulged only child, was about to lose my mother. What a terrible time to wed! And then, of course, Andrew was a trapper, a man who liked his rough cabin deep in the forest. His notion of a good life didn't necessarily include staying home in a grand house."

"You said you aren't a widow," I ventured. "Did you get a . . . a divorce?" I knew the word, from novels. But I didn't know a soul who actually *had* divorced, or a family that admitted one in its farthest branches.

"No. That would have shocked even me. Andrew was a good man. He and I just didn't suit. He stayed until Mother died, then he left me here to care for Father while he made a trapping excursion into the Michigan Territories. We'd planned it out. When he had traveled far from Ohio, he sent a letter informing me of Andrew Mercer's death. I became a widow in the sight of the village. He rechristened himself Mark Andrews and continued to trap and explore and live on the edge of the frontier."

"So that's why you haven't remarried," I said. "You don't know if your husband is dead or alive."

"Oh, he's alive, all right. We remain friends in an odd way. I get messages from him now and again. Several bundles of furs have arrived over the years. Why, just last spring I received a package from California, of all places. My *cousin*, Mark Andrews, had found a big strike and wanted to share his good fortune. Gold nuggets, resting safely in the bank just now."

"But you couldn't remarry. . . ."

"Wouldn't want to." She laughed. "You young girls. Romance fills your heads and you never see what comes after. Perhaps I saw too clearly, losing Mother as I did. Marriage can bring a woman's downfall. She loses her independence, her property. Her health and energy, too. That's not for me. Father hadn't taken the time to deed the farm to Andrew at our marriage because Mother was so sick. As time passed, I think he had suspicions, and he wrote his will so that both farms became mine alone, to do with as I chose."

My head whirled. Widow Mercer has lived such a complicated life. I doubt any of the townspeople know a word of this story.

"What made you tell me?" I asked at last. My tea had grown cold in its cup and the gingerbread sat uneaten.

"I don't quite know," she admitted. "Your confusion about your young men, perhaps. I detect a spark of rebelliousness in you, Lucinda. A spark I would encourage into flame. Or maybe I'm simply growing older and want to share my past. Seeing Cass so ill, it brings back the bad times, when I lost Mother.

"Anyway, I've finished this drawing and you may look. Actually, I've finished several in this afternoon's long talk. Perhaps they'll cheer Cass." She passed me her sketchbook.

I opened the first page and felt a lightning shock. She'd captured me as I sat at the table and stitched, wearing a faraway, dreamy smile on my face. She had looked right into my heart, for as she told about her romance with Andrew Mercer, I'd thought about Jeremiah Strong.

I couldn't bear to look anymore. She'd come too close. I flipped the page and saw portraits—Ben and Shad making snowballs, Emma nursing baby Lizzie, Naomi and Ruth sitting close together as they listened to their naming story, Daniel and Mesha eating pie. In each picture the people seemed ready to speak, to laugh.

"You're amazing," I said at last. "The most unusual woman I've ever met."

I admire her unconventional life, but I also find her unnerving. For with those artist's eyes of hers, Miss Aurelia sees too much.

TUESDAY, FEBRUARY 11, 1851

The noise of horses woke me from a sound sleep in the small hours this morning. I tensed. Was it someone coming to search the house? Visions of Clayton Roberts's evil blue eyes crossed my brain. I listened, hoping the sound would grow faint, but instead it came closer. I rapped on Miss Aurelia's door and warned her.

A whistle shrilled through the icy night air and I relaxed. William. I grabbed a shawl and ran downstairs to greet my brother. "We waited so long! Are they safe? How was your trip? Is Jeremiah with you? Did the snow hold you up?"

I hugged him, and he hugged me back, surprising me with the strength of his arms. My brother was fast turning into a man.

"Jeremiah and I saw them onto the lake steamer, bound for Windsor, Canada West. With the snow, we stayed in Cleveland—in the house of a family of Quakers Jeremiah knows."

"Thank the Lord," Miss Aurelia whispered. "William, come and warm yourself. We'll tell Cass your news."

"I have something for her," Will said. He patted his pocket.

Up in the attic, Cass was awake. My candle caught a

fearful look on her face. The noises had disturbed her sleep, too.

I sat beside her. "Cass, your family is in Canada. They're safe. Free!"

"Glory be!" She sat up, and her face glowed. Her eyes shone with unshed tears. "Tell me."

"The trip north went smooth," Will said. "We made Cleveland by Tuesday morning. We sheltered with Abraham in a fish warehouse near the lake. Did that stink! When it got dark, we smuggled the children on board the steamer. I loaned Emma a set of my clothes, and we all made like dockworkers. We set each child in an empty fish barrel and hauled them on board like salt perch. The captain saw them all safe, landed on Canada soil."

He reached into his pocket and pulled out a piece of paper. "A Baptist church sits close by the docks in Windsor. Go there for help. Abraham and Emma will have a place by the time you arrive. They'll leave word at the church so that you can find their house."

Will passed the paper to Cass, and she held it to her chest like a great treasure. "My babies. They free! God be praised."

Miss Aurelia took her hands. "Yes, thanks be to God. Now let's get you well and this youngster born."

"Yes, Miss Aurelia. I do what you say. My babies free. This child and me, we join them real soon."

She took hold of Will's hand. "Thank you," she said. "You just a boy, but you man enough to carry my babies to the promised land."

Will shrugged. His face turned bright red.

"You a brave boy, and a strong one," she said.

We went downstairs, and Miss Aurelia and I fed Will plate after plate of hot food.

"Never thought I'd get warm," he said. "Trip up, the roads were muddy but not bad. Good thing we had a place to stay in Cleveland till the first snow wore itself out. The roads home weren't no prize."

"It snowed a lot?"

"Yep. 'Specially up by Lake Erie. And it drifted. I'd get patches of dry road, and then places where Jeremiah and me had to dig for an hour to go a quarter mile. Then more snow came on Saturday."

"Is Jeremiah home, too?"

"Should be," Will said. He passed me an envelope. "He sent you a letter. I don't suppose you'll read it out loud."

I snatched the letter from Will's hand and blushed furiously.

"Would you stay here the night, William?" Miss Aurelia offered.

"Thank you, ma'am, but Mama will turn blue with worry if I'm gone much longer. I brought some fish, if you'd like, and I'll carry news to Mama and Papa. Do you need anything? Supplies?"

How could Will rattle on about fish and supplies? I counted the minutes until I could rush upstairs and read Jeremiah's letter.

"Fresh fish sounds nice, but otherwise we're fine," Miss Aurelia said. "Unless you'd like to go home now, Lucinda. I can manage on my own with just Cass for a bit. I'm sure your mother misses you."

I tugged my thoughts away from Jeremiah. What had

she said? Home. Did I want to go home? Absolutely. Now that I'd seen Will, I wanted the rest of my family close around me. But Cass worried me. I couldn't leave until her child was born. "I still think it's safer with two of us here," I said. "If Cass has trouble, I can ride for help."

"Yes, but a day or two won't hurt, surely."

"I'll think about it. But not tonight."

I wasn't ready to say goodbye yet, but I knew Will had to go home. Mama and Papa needed to see his face and hear his story.

I hugged him again, and as I passed him my latest letters for the family I fingered the one from Jeremiah. Another night without much sleep, but I didn't mind in the least this time.

7 *February*

Dear Lucinda,

By the time this reaches thee, I will be safe in our inn with Father, Mother, and my sister and brothers. Thee, on the other hand, will still be hard at work. Know that the temptation grows in me to visit Sister Mercer's farm. Only the seriousness of her condition keeps me away. Too many days have passed since we last spoke. And this journey, unlike the last, was passed in company, so I have had less time and privacy to write thee.

I scribble this from Cleveland, where I wait out a storm with thy brother. He's a good lad, that Will Spencer. Young but broad-shouldered, willing to take on great burdens. Thy family must be pleased with him.

As I am sure he has told thee, our trading expedition here has met with success, and I look forward to concluding the deliveries as soon as we can arrange it. These winter journeys both chill and invigorate. I would love to share one with thee. How might we arrange such a thing? Am I too bold to ask?

Perhaps when Sister Mercer has regained her health, thee would permit me to come calling. Or I could help thee travel back to thy home. I admit it, Lucinda, thee has caught my heart in thy hands and thy face appears often before me. So please, allow me to visit thee soon.

Until then, I am

Thy faithful Friend,
Jeremiah Strong

WEDNESDAY, FEBRUARY 12, 1851

CASS BABIES FREE!

HALLELU!

Today Cass and I worked, hard as ever, but with light hearts—she because she knew her family was safe, I because of Jeremiah's letter.

"You seem better today, Cass. Are your legs still swollen?"

"My soul fly like some bird, Lucy. But this old baby still wear out my body. My legs hurt. My heart, it hurry sometimes, then it slow down again. Here, you feel it."

I felt for the pulse at her neck. The speed of her heartbeat scared me. I cut our lessons short and talked her into a longer nap, since we'd been up well into the night.

I told Miss Aurelia about Cass's heart racing.

"We'd better get help," she said. "Even though the baby's not coming yet, it wouldn't hurt for Bessie to check on Cass."

"I'll ride over and get her," I offered. "I'm worried." That was true. What I didn't say was that a ride gave me a glorious chance to go outdoors, free of the house, if only for an hour or so.

I hurried upstairs and changed, pulling on long woolen underwear, thick stockings, a knitted vest, and the knickers and woolen jacket I use at night. With boots, mittens, and a cap, I'd look more like Tom or Will than myself, but I'd also ride warm and comfortable.

Miss Aurelia helped me saddle up one of her horses, and I cantered off easily across frozen fields. I avoided the drifted snow and let the mare make her own way toward the Smith's farm. Wind cut through my clothing, but the sun warmed my back and I jogged along happily. For while I traveled on a serious mission, my thoughts returned again and again to Jeremiah Strong. He had written. He would come to call. I wanted to sing aloud. The ride ended much too soon.

Mrs. Smith welcomed me into her warm kitchen with a wide smile and a firm handshake. She is a small woman, with medium brown skin and black hair braided in the African manner in neat rows along her head. She served me bread and cheese and tea as I explained about Cass.

"She's how big? How far along?"

I shrugged and held my arms in a wide circle around my own waist. "Big. I don't know. Her legs pain her. They've swelled up. She says a few weeks still."

"First baby?"

"No, third. But she had this trouble with the others, too."

She nodded. "I'll see to her."

I needed to tell Mrs. Smith more about Cass. I needed to warn her. I took a deep breath. "Mrs. Smith, you should know . . . she's a runaway. Come only if you can risk it."

"I know already. And if I don't risk it, who will? How you think I got here, gal? Some wood creatures brought me? I came from down Virginia as a young woman, following my man. Someone risked it for me years back. Many someones, colored and white. Lord be praised, they stopped looking for me a long time ago, so I can stay here. But I'll never forget my journey." Her black eyes drilled into me, and fire rose to her brown-gold cheeks.

I felt like a thoughtless child. "I'm sorry. I only meant to warn you, so you'd be cautious."

"I understand cautious," she said, and gave me a forgiving smile. "Now, I can't come right today. My littlest has a croupy cough. But I'll send you back with remedies, some herbs to make into a tea. Should ease the pain and swelling without harming the babe."

She handed me a packet and showed me how much to use, and then another, larger bundle.

"Mix this up with hot water in a poultice and put it

on her chest. Wrap a flannel around it. Do that morning and evening."

I didn't understand. "Why her chest, if her legs are swollen?"

"Heart's pumping too fast, sounds like. We need to slow that down. You're keeping her in bed now, aren't you?"

"Yes, ma'am. Ever since she arrived."

"Good. You get started. I'll stop over in a day or two, at most."

"Could you come sooner? Miss Aurelia and I . . . we've never done this before and we don't know exactly when the baby will come. . . ."

Mrs. Smith laughed. "Nobody knows *exactly* when a baby'll come. I've birthed three myself and welcomed many others, so between us we'll bring that child into the world just fine. Don't you worry now. I'll see your visitor soon enough."

"All right. Thank you, Mrs. Smith." She reached up and patted my cheek to send me on my way. I felt foolish again.

Mrs. Smith is so tiny, but her calm confidence makes her seem bigger. I'll sure welcome that confidence when Cass starts her labor. When it comes to birthing babies, I am a complete and total child, and unfortunately, so is Miss Aurelia.

THURSDAY, FEBRUARY 13, 1851

The herbs Mrs. Smith sent make a minty-smelling tea. Cass seems to like it well enough. The poultice stinks, but

Cass doesn't complain. Fact is, she doesn't complain about much, while I always grouch about the stitching. I finished those swaddling blankets and now sew on a baby quilt made from scraps while she practices names of her family on an old slate of Miss Aurelia's.

"Ouch! Dratted needle! And now I've tangled the thread." I threw down the cloth.

Cass picked it up and tugged gently at the knots. In no time she had the cloth and thread smooth and ready to sew again. "How'd you do that? I usually have to cut out the knots and start over."

She laughed at me. "All you got to do is follow the thread, one knot at a time. You in too big a hurry, Lucy."

"Well, I want the quilt done by the time the baby comes. Besides, I'm not good at going slow, with sewing or anything else. I doubt I could wait a whole nine months for a child myself. Is it hard work, having a baby?" I asked.

She laughed again and shook her head at me. "Hard work, yes. But better than old tobacco farming. End of that job, we get a mess of stinky leaves. End of this job, I get a little child to love." She patted her big belly. "Ain't that better?"

"Lots. I remember when every one of my brothers and sister came. Mama worked real hard, but the babies were sweet."

"Every baby in the world be sweet," she said. "Even if . . ." She stopped and sighed.

"What, Cass?"

"Even if I don't like they daddy," she said, her voice so quiet I could barely hear.

"Emma told me. I'm sorry, Cass. But you'll get free. That man can't hurt you anymore. I'll take you to Canada myself. In Canada you can pick your own husband, for love."

She sighed. "I be hearing you, Lucy. But the master, he pester me so long . . . Some days I feel a hundred years old."

"But you're nineteen. That's just three years older than I am."

"Three years free time, hundred years slave time," she said.

Now what in the name of Sunday is a person supposed to reply to that?

FRIDAY, FEBRUARY 14, 1851

Mrs. Smith came and went. She won't say when the child will be born, except "a while." Cass didn't mind much, but I did. Bah! This is worse than waiting for Christmas. And I'm sick of snow!

SATURDAY, FEBRUARY 15, 1851

Cass thrives at her studies. It keeps me from going mad with boredom. I'm writing out lessons for her to carry north and share with the rest of the family, so I'm not completely useless.

And Cass started giving me lessons. She studied the quilt I stitched on and tore out nearly half. "You work too fast, Lucy. Here, I show you." I hope she'll improve more with her pens and papers than I will with my needle and thread. For she's right, of course. I'm more interested in how fast I'll finish than in making each little stitch smooth and perfect.

Bah on February. The month is halfway gone. How much waiting can a person endure? I must have asked that question out loud, for Cass answered.

"Depend on the person," she said. Then she laughed at me.

"All right. I admit, I deserve it. But must you laugh so hard?"

Her laughing was more catching than measles, and soon we both held our bellies. It feels good to have a friend to talk to again.

SUNDAY, FEBRUARY 16, 1851

That man! How could I have ever thought him handsome? He is wretched. And conniving!

That dreadful Clayton Roberts came here, right up to Miss Aurelia's door. To see me! And him a married man with all those children. He has no morals at all!

"Good day to you, Miss Lucy," he said as I opened the door.

"Mr. Roberts?" What was he doing here? Heaven help us if he wanted to search the house today. I had no time to warn anybody.

"Yep. Back here again. I've been riding all over northern Ohio, looking for my property. But something . . . something keeps calling me back to this sweet little town."

Something. Did he somehow guess Cass was hiding up

in the attic? Or was I the something? Either choice was terrible.

"You weren't in church this mornin'," he drawled. He stomped the snow from his boots, as though he expected to be invited inside. "I asked about you, and they told me you were still helping the widow. Those measles seem to be bothering her a right long time."

I scowled. "She's had complications. Coughing. Fevers come and go. If you'll excuse me . . ."

He stuck his foot in the door so I couldn't slam it in his face. "I just hate to see such a sweet young gal shut up here for weeks at a time. I'd hoped your invalid might be well enough for you to come for a ride with me. You're looking so pale, Miss Lucy."

"I'm always pale, sir. It goes with red hair. And no, Miss Aurelia's condition will not permit me to leave her to go off riding with a stranger. I cannot even consider your invitation. Good day."

I banged the door shut, hoping to catch his dratted foot and bruise it. I'd had to bite my tongue nearly in two to keep from shouting that I knew he was married and that he had a mistress and a passel of children.

Long after he'd gone, I stared at the door and wondered how many men were slimy snakes like Clayton Roberts.

MONDAY, FEBRUARY 17, 1851
LATE AFTERNOON

Visitors, two days in a row. Did someone send out invitations without telling us? Today's batch caught me in the barn. The stalls needed mucking out, and I craved the exercise. I still fumed from yesterday.

When I heard horses I hurried inside to warn Miss Aurelia. I tried hard to keep my voice steady, but fear crept up my spine like a deadly spider. Had Clayton Roberts come back? And who was he after, Cass or me?

Miss Aurelia nodded. "Thanks, Lucy. I'll bang the ceiling so Cass will know, then I'll arrange myself as a convalescent in the parlor. You go on about the chores—take on the hard work while I recuperate." She coughed, as if disease had settled into her lungs, then winked at me. I hoped her courage would rub off, for mine had disappeared.

I stood on the front porch and watched the road. The horse noises came closer, and soon I made out the shape of a closed trap. Clayton Roberts had driven such a trap yesterday, worse luck.

I trudged toward the barn and hoped the trap would keep rolling, hoped it had a different destination, but the horses turned up Miss Aurelia's lane. We had visitors coming, wanted or not. I squinted into the sun, trying to discover who.

A woman's voice called out. "Hello, Lucinda! We've come to call on Widow Mercer."

Relief. Only Mrs. Cummings. But she'd said *we*—I wished furiously that she hadn't brought her daughter, Eleanora. I scowled. If the person with Mrs. Cummings was old, a church lady, I could probably stay outside.

The horses drew up to the barn and I saw Mrs. Cummings and Mrs. Clark, Jonathan's mother. Hallelujah! No catchers. No Eleanora.

I walked toward the trap and found my voice. "Hello, ladies."

Mrs. Clark tossed me the reins as if I were a stable boy. "We've come to see the widow. She's over the measles by now, isn't she? It's been weeks. We expected you in church yesterday."

I ignored the scolding and hitched the team to the porch railing. "The spots have faded. But she has a touch of lung congestion and fever. Every time she breathes this cold air, she gets a fit of coughing, so I do the outside chores."

"Poor Aurelia," Mrs. Cummings said with a shake of her head. She climbed down from her seat and hefted a large basket. "With one thing and another, the woman's been visited with more plagues than the Egyptians. And I doubt she's been as wicked as they were."

She paused, and I lifted her basket to the porch. "You know, Lucinda, my husband preached on that very text this week. Pity you and Aurelia missed such a good sermon."

Pity? I'd say not. Missing the Reverend's tedious sermons has been a treat for me. But I'll never tell his wife. "Have a lovely visit. Nice of you to come." I turned toward the barn.

"Surely you'll visit with us," Mrs. Clark said. She smiled, but I didn't like the way she ordered me around.

"I'm sorry. I have to see to the animals. Snow makes them restless."

"Surely they can wait an hour," she said. Her thin nose rose in the air and she frowned.

"I'm sorry," I repeated. I waved to them and bit my

lip to keep a fool's smile off my face until I reached the barn.

Once inside, I drew the doors shut before huge laughs burst out of me. The cows mooed and the horses whinnied in reply. Dear Lord—if those biddies only knew what we were up to, or if they suspected the wild things I knew about Miss Aurelia! Mrs. Cummings would bust out of her corset and Mrs. Clark's nose would grow an inch.

I shed my coat and set to work on the first cow's stall, humming as I worked. "Thank you, cows, for making such a mess," I said aloud, then bent into another fit of laughter. I wondered how long the ladies would stay and plague Miss Aurelia.

I'd mucked out four stalls and given my favorite mare a good brushing before I heard the noise of harness and chatter. I replaced the pitchfork and tidied the barn, hoping they'd leave right away.

But Mrs. Clark didn't let me escape. She shoved open the barn door and studied the stalls. "A girl of many talents. Industrious. I like that. Here, Lucinda. My son sent you a letter."

I stood by the barn and watched them drive off.

Miss Aurelia met me at the front door. She wore a smile as big as the moon. "Lucinda, you've got straw in your hair."

"Mucky boots, too. I'll wash up and check on Cass. Then you must tell me everything."

She chuckled. "For that we'll need a fresh pot of tea."

I left my boots on the back porch and hurried upstairs

to wash. Cass was glad to hear that the visitors were gone. She looked tired out, so I didn't stay long.

Miss Aurelia had a steaming pot of tea and a plate of apple cake waiting when I returned, clean, to the kitchen.

"They're good cooks," she said. "We'll take two days off." She cut a wide slice of apple cake for me and set it next to my teacup.

"What happened? They stayed forever." I sat to eat.

"Well, they sympathized with my illness. Once they'd started, though, the stories flew like the snow. If I'd really felt ill, I think the tales of old lady Watkins's boils might have set my recovery back a good month."

I laughed. "Old lady Watkins has boils?" I stirred my tea.

Miss Aurelia blinked and stuck her nose in the air. "I won't tell you where. But I can say she doesn't sit comfortably these days." Her voice and manner imitated Mrs. Clark perfectly.

"How about the Reverend's wife?"

"Mary Martha behaved well. The Lord gave her a load of common sense. She was kind—cool water on a sunburned arm. As opposed to the other one."

"You don't like Mrs. Clark, do you?"

Miss Aurelia's forehead wrinkled like she needed to think out her opinion. "I had the strangest feeling that she came here for a reason entirely unrelated to my illness."

I dropped my fork. "Not Cass?"

Miss Aurelia frowned again and added fresh tea to our cups. "No. It was the oddest thing, Lucy. She wandered.

Said she was putting away the food. But I watched her run her finger across the parlor table, checking for crumbs. And she asked questions about you. How was your cooking? Had you kept the house tidy? Had you scorched anything when you ironed? She was investigating *you*."

I groaned.

"What?" A smile teased at the corner of Miss Aurelia's mouth.

"She nosed all around the barn, too."

"Investigating you for a daughter-in-law?" Miss Aurelia asked.

I scowled.

Miss Aurelia laughed. "When Cass wakes, we'll take a piece of this excellent apple cake up to her."

"Perhaps I'll drop crumbs on the way," I said, mischief welling up inside. "Or jostle some of your lovely pictures. I'm afraid I'll make a terrible housekeeper."

MONDAY, FEBRUARY 17, 1851
EVENING

Some trace of that mischief must have showed in my face, for Cass grinned when I entered the attic with her dinner and the cake.

"What you been doing, Lucy? You looking like that rascal Shad when he snitch peaches from the master's trees."

"I'm laughing about the church ladies," I began. I explained about Jonathan and his nosy mother. "We think she was inspecting me. To see if I'm good enough to marry her son."

"You plenty good for anybody," Cass said firmly. "I wonder, do this boy be good enough for you?"

Her eyes blazed, and I thought again how different our situations were.

"What else, Lucy? Something hide in your eyes. You gonna tell me or make me guess?"

I reached into my pocket for the newest letter from Jonathan. "Hold on. This won't make sense unless I read you the first two he wrote. And I have to explain what happened. It could take a while. . . ."

"Get the letter, Lucy. I ain't going noplace."

I did. And when I returned, I told her about kissing Jeremiah by the fire. Then I read Jonathan's first two letters aloud.

"He don't got sense," she said. "All that fussing for just a kiss." She fluffed her pillow so she could sit up. "What happen next?"

"I wrote and said I'd been too busy to think. Said I was sorry."

Cass laughed. "Men! They believe most anything. Well, let 'em. It don't hurt you or me to have a little secret held back. You going to read that other letter or just wave it at me?"

I grinned and opened the envelope. "Listen to this. . . ."

Dear Lucinda,

I received your letter and thought about it for a long time. I realize you are busy and you have been holding up well with the strain of caring for Widow Mercer.

I suppose I shall forgive your flirtation with the Quaker if you promise me it will never happen again. I think it will be best if we mend our affections when you are rested, for I find myself uncertain about meanings in letters. I wonder what you are thinking.

"You think him a fool, that's what," Cass interrupted.

"Oh, Cass," I protested. "I'm trying to be fair. I liked him for a long time. Let me read the rest."

The difficult part was seeing you kiss him. I can't block that vision from my mind. And Lucinda, if somehow the moon and the firelight led you astray once, might they not do so again? If you really liked me, how could you kiss him and enjoy it?

"He right about that, Lucy? You like kissing that Quaker man?"

My cheeks burned. "Yes. I liked it. A lot."

"More than you like kissing the one who write the sour letter?"

"Lots more."

"Kiss him again," she said, smiling. "Kiss the Quaker man again."

"Cass!"

"Ain't that what you been wanting to do all these days?"

I looked at the floor, unable to meet her gaze.

"Well, ain't it, Lucy? I remember what good kissing feel like, even if it happen a long time back. You listen to your heart, gal."

"Right now I have to read this letter. It gets worse."

Cass nodded as I returned to the page.

As I read this I realize I sound unforgiving. But I'm trying not to be. And I must admit I'm not entirely blameless. I will confess that after I saw you out by the fire, I grew angry and tried to push you from my mind. I spent most of the evening dancing with Eleanora Cummings. She's a very pretty girl, you know. And so I kissed her, several times. Perhaps we're on equal footing, Lucinda. But when I kissed Eleanora, I didn't really enjoy it. Angry kisses aren't sweet. I like sweet ones better. I hope you and I can forgive each other and heal this rift in our affections. Until I see you again, I am,

Your loving, if confused,
Jonathan

The letter fell to my lap. "I feel so dumb. I don't really like him anymore, but this letter still makes me mad."

"We ain't always smart," Cass said gently.

"It isn't fair, Cass," I said. "Men seem to think they have different rules than women. It's all right for him to kiss her, but not for me to kiss Jeremiah? Well, he won't be kissing me anymore."

"Good for you, Lucy." She smiled; then her face took on a serious look. "Where I come from, men do what they want. Nobody can stop them. Old Roberts, he take a shine to me, so he have me. His wife don't like it, but what can she do? What can I do?"

"You did what you could. You ran away. That's about the bravest thing in the world. You risked your life for freedom."

Cass shrugged. "Sometimes I wonder. It ain't never really been my life. Not till we run. I always belong to somebody else. I never get to choose nothing. Don't call me brave, Lucy. I just try to take hold of my life before somebody use it all up."

Cass looked tired. I straightened her quilt and squeezed her hand, then left so she could sleep again. But her words stick with me. Is that what girls and women have to do, the world over? Do we have to take hold of our lives before somebody else uses them all up?

<small>Tuesday, February 18, 1851</small>

Mama says trouble often comes in threes. But today didn't bring trouble, it brought Mama herself! Hallelujah! If I weren't taller than she is, I'd have climbed right into her lap and stayed there like a tiny child. I sure did hug her a lot, and cried, too.

Miss Aurelia left us alone, and Mama caught me up on family news. Well, there wasn't really much news, but we talked away half the day. When I asked her about the ironing that she'd put off to visit, she said something so un-Mama-like, I nearly slid off my chair.

"I'd wear wrinkles for the rest of my life if it meant getting you home sooner, Lucy dear. I've missed you dreadfully."

And I've missed her, but . . . This doesn't make sense, but here is the place where I put the truth. So I will write, and maybe I'll understand afterward.

Some odd part of me wishes Mama hadn't come to visit. I miss my family a lot, bushelsful and bushelsful. But today, since she's come and gone again, I miss her a hundred times worse.

Enough feeling sorry for myself. I'll read the letter Mama brought from Rebecca.

13 *February*

Dear Lucinda,

First things first. Here is my prank—when it gets warm enough to sneak out at night, we'll load a wagon with straw on a Saturday night and carry it to the church after dark.

(I know for a fact the Reverend and his family go to sleep early on Saturday nights so that he'll be rested for Sunday services. Perhaps it might improve his sermons if he were more sleepless. Who knows?)

We'll climb the church tower with loads of straw and stuff it into the church bell. Then on Sunday morning, when Mr. Marshall pulls the rope—nothing!

Now, we have two choices. We can do this ourselves, or we can invite our young men to help. Do Quakers pull pranks? I vote for an all-girls excursion, but you decide.

Lucy! Your new romance is amazing. Jonathan Clark is a dear boy, but we have known him forever. And his mother is a terror.

But Jeremiah Strong? Oh, Lucy, he's very handsome in a stern sort of way. But a Quaker? How do they behave, anyway? My mother would never allow me to keep company with someone so different. Or so old. He's nearly twenty, isn't he?

I hope your parents will understand better than mine would. As for me, whomever you choose, I will approve and wish you well.

Now you must do just that for me. Nathaniel has spoken to

Father! He has permission to come calling. Privately, of course, we talk of more than that, but I think it's wise to break the news to parents a bit at a time and not worry them too much. So while we are not officially engaged, we have had talks about someday.

Here is what someday looks like. (And no, Lucy, I'm not like you. I don't crave surprises unless it's a prank. I prefer plans.) Nathaniel has spoken with a Quaker man in Salem. His name is Eli Whitman—you've probably heard that he was caught aiding a runaway slave and that the magistrate found him guilty. Shocking, isn't it, that someone we know is involved in such things?

Friend Whitman hasn't been sent to jail, but he must sell his farm to pay his fines. His neighbors are so cruel, he plans to pick up and move to Indiana and start afresh.

Nathaniel and his father are arranging to buy the farm from Friend Whitman. When Nathaniel has paid a good part of the purchase, the farm will be ours, Nathaniel's and mine! We will turn twenty in four years, and that seems a good age to marry, doesn't it? Please agree. And promise you'll stand with me when we marry, for you are my sweetest and dearest friend.

Part of me worries that I'll benefit from someone's distress, but I console my conscience by promising to take wonderful care of the house (it's a beauty) and the farm. I hope the Whitmans feel they can leave their home in good hands with Nathaniel and me. And they have broken the law, so perhaps leaving is a good idea. The whole issue confuses me, but people can be unkind.

Lucy, dear, what do you think? Write back and tell me right away, for I haven't shared these someday plans with anyone else. I'm bursting to talk with you. I shall pray hard for

Widow Mercer to recover so that you can return to being my truest friend.

Fondly,
Rebecca

I'll go home soon. And a good thing, for if I have time to ponder Rebecca's letter, I'll grow gloomy and discouraged. Can my dearest friend in the world disapprove of our work on the Railroad? Can she truly find Quakers too different? I pray not.

The snow began again this morning, and I scurried to bring in extra firewood and complete the barn work before it got too deep. Miss Aurelia stayed inside, cooked, and watched Cass. After the chores were done, I hauled extra water. I also built up the fire so that we could start supper early.

But when Miss Aurelia came down from the attic that afternoon, supper wasn't on her mind. "Cass is laboring," she said. "Her time has come, and it's earlier than we thought. How bad is that snow, Lucy? Can you ride for Bessie Smith?"

Where had the weeks gone? They'd melted into days, but I wasn't sorry. "I'll go right away."

Snow flew everywhere, in my face, across the road, down my neck. The only warmth I could feel came from Miss Aurelia's dependable mare. I had wanted adventure but hadn't imagined such a cold one.

When I reached the house, Mrs. Smith readied herself in a moment and we turned our horses toward Miss Aurelia's. We rode side by side, heads bent into the wind, a rope looped between our saddles for safety. The wind blew in from the northwest, a lake storm that dumped more and more snow across our backs. Our horses' manes and tails turned white.

"Perhaps we should turn back," Mrs. Smith shouted. "I can't see the road."

"Cass needs us. We have to go on," I called. "If we follow the line of trees and fence posts, we won't get lost."

I wriggled my toes, but they didn't have much feeling. I blew warm breath into my mittens. Clouds thickened overhead and the afternoon grew dark. I squinted into the white swirl. The trees that marked the road faded into blurry shadows. I nearly bumped into one as we veered across the road. I corrected our direction and peered into the distance for a lantern light but saw only blowing snow.

It seemed like hours later when we finally saw lights from Miss Aurelia's windows. I tended the horses while Mrs. Smith hurried inside. Blood and warmth returned to my fingers and toes as I rubbed down the horses, then fed and watered them, giving each an extra measure of oats as a reward. From the noises I heard in the stalls, Miss Aurelia hadn't had time to milk her cows, so I completed that chore, warming more as I leaned into the solid bulk of each cow.

I felt no great hurry to enter the house. Childbirth is mysterious, frightening. I worried for Cass, but my mind saw Mama's mournful face after she lost that baby boy. I'd have stayed with the animals for the night, but my stomach growled and I couldn't very well eat oats. So I made my way, with brimming pails of milk, through the snow and wind to Miss Aurelia's kitchen.

She stood at the stove and added water to a kettle. "Oh, Lucy. You've milked. What with tending Cass, I plain forgot the poor cows."

"They're fine. How is Cass?"

"She says she's not going to have this baby after all—it's all a big mistake. Bessie says laboring women get odd notions like that, and it means Cass is pretty far along. Good thing I never had to go through childbirth. My temperament isn't given to patience."

I grinned and shrugged off my damp coat.

"Water's hot. I'll brew you some tea and set aside a basin for washing. You look all done in from the ride, Lucy."

"Thanks." I traded the milk pails for a basin and hurried up. It felt good to strip off my wet clothing and wash with warm water. As I buttoned up my clean dress I heard Cass cry out. My heart thudded with the sound, so like Mama when she was in labor last spring.

I finished dressing and hurried up to where Mrs. Smith sat next to Cass, rubbing her back. "How are you doing?" I whispered to Cass.

"I be tired, Lucy. Plain old tired. But I glad you got this lady to help. Didn't know what I'd do without Emma."

"She's doing fine," Mrs. Smith said. "The pains come and go, but that's normal."

I nodded as if I knew what she was talking about and ducked back down the stairs. I didn't want to be around if Cass yelled again. It was one thing to ride out in a snowstorm for help; I could handle that kind of adventure. But sit next to a birthing bed and help, or even watch? Please, no. I'd probably faint dead away and need nursing myself.

In the kitchen, Miss Aurelia had fried up bacon and scrambled eggs. The smells made my mouth water. We sat to eat, and I ate like my brothers—second helpings heaped high. "You'd think I'd been starved for days," I said when I'd cleaned the last bite of eggs from the plate.

"It's the cold," Miss Aurelia said. "And the excitement. You burned a lot of energy this afternoon. You needed a good hot meal."

"What about Mrs. Smith? Won't she need food, too? Somebody could stay with Cass while she eats." I hoped the somebody wouldn't be me. "And Cass. She's working harder than any of us. She must be starving."

"Cass can't eat. Bessie says so. Bessie had tea and biscuits when she first got here. We'll spell her from time to time so she gets a chance to rest and eat."

"All right. I'll help."

Miss Aurelia smiled. "Excited about this, aren't you, Lucy?"

"I'd rather chop wood," I admitted. "I want the baby to come. And I want Cass to be all right. But pain and bleeding make me dizzy."

"My thoughts exactly," Miss Aurelia said. "I'm so grateful you could ride for Bessie. Imagine if we'd had to do this all ourselves."

"Poor Cass. Imagine if she had to depend on just us." I shook my head as more noise came from above. "I don't want to think about it," I said. "Don't you have something for me to do? Washing or baking?"

"I've already started bread," she said. "But if you want to clear up these dishes, I surely wouldn't mind."

Miss Aurelia tiptoed up to check on Cass, and I set to work at the sink. I scrubbed each plate, fork, and spoon at least three times. I rinsed and dried the dishes until they shone. I attacked the skillet, scraping egg from the sides. But that took only a few minutes.

I wish we'd fed fifty people, or a hundred, so I'd have something to occupy my hands. I'm a lot like Miss Aurelia: God left patience off my list of virtues. I can't help but question if I'll ever be a mother myself. First you have to wait nine months for the child to grow, then the birthing takes forever. And from the sounds, it hurts like the dickens. Maybe I'm just plain dumb or I've missed something important, but with all the trouble it takes to have children, it seems a miracle the human race has survived.

Poor Cass. Her life has been hard enough. Please, God, give her this baby quick and make it healthy and safe. Amen.

THURSDAY, FEBRUARY 20, 1851

The birth of Hope!

It sounds like a biblical event. I wore out my knees, praying all night. But the waiting is over. Hallelujah, everybody is fine!

Dawn pinked the sky when we finally heard the soft, mewing cry that told us the baby was born.

Miss Aurelia and I hurried with supplies. She had towels and warm water. I carried the bundle of little clothes I'd made, with my favorite yellow flannel gown and blanket on top.

I'd expected Cass to look like she'd been beaten up, but instead she smiled at us. "Congratulations, Cass!" I said. "A boy or a girl?"

"Girl. I name her Hope," she said, her voice strong and proud. "She the hope of our family. First one born free."

I squeezed Cass's hand, then turned to Mrs. Smith, who held Hope in her arms. My breath caught as I looked into that tiny face. Her nose was no bigger than my thumb, her eyes shone like black marbles, and her curly dark hair was soft and damp as moss when I touched it.

"She's beautiful, Cass." My spine tingled as I touched the tiny hand. She grabbed on to my finger and held tight. "She's a strong one," I said. "If she hangs on to her freedom the way she's hanging on to me, she'll earn her name and more. Can I wash and dress her? I've helped Mama a lot."

Mrs. Smith passed Hope to me. "Sure enough. She's a good strong baby, all right. Mind the cord."

I held her close and she curled into me, warm and sweet.

Once she'd passed me the baby Mrs. Smith bustled around Cass, and it amazed me. I'd drowsed on and off all night while she'd worked straight through yet her energy put me to shame. Miss Aurelia stepped in to give her a hand, and I took charge of dressing the baby.

Hope looked all red and wrinkled, but everything was perfect, from her tiny toes to the soft fuzz on her head.

Her skin was paler than I'd expected, but then I remembered Ruth and Mesha and their white father. I washed and dressed her quickly and wrapped her snug in the flannel blanket so she'd stay warm. I got to hold her for a few minutes more while Miss Aurelia and Mrs. Smith changed the bedsheets around Cass, sponged her off, and put a fresh nightgown on her. Mrs. Smith placed her hand near Cass's heart and waited a moment, then tucked in mother and baby for a rest.

We made our way downstairs to the kitchen for breakfast.

"She's all right?" Miss Aurelia asked.

"Baby's fine," Mrs. Smith said. "Watch the mother for a day or two. Her condition is tender. Her heart pumps faster than I'd like. It should calm once she gets some rest, but keep somebody with her for at least two days."

"I'll help," I offered. Now that the birthing was through and we had a sweet baby to fuss over, I'd do anything.

"We'll take turns," Miss Aurelia said. "We did extra chores last night, so we can rest today." She pushed back a curtain, and pale early sunlight shone through. "Why is it babies always get born in the middle of a storm? Are they just naturally cantankerous? If she'd waited until today, your trip would have been a sight easier."

Mrs. Smith laughed. "Babies don't care about easier," she said. "At least I'll have a nice ride home."

"Shall I come along?"

"I'll do fine once I get a good breakfast in me. My African blood needs fortifying for these northern winters. You tend to Cass and I'll ride along on my own."

We had a quiet day at Miss Aurelia's. I slept in the morning while Miss Aurelia finished up the last of her chores and watched over Cass. She woke me for midday dinner, and I took charge while she rested, but it hardly felt like work. We'd pulled a rocking chair up to the attic, and I sat there and read some of Mr. Hawthorne's stories while Cass and the baby slept the afternoon away. My only labor was warming up the remains of dinner for our evening meal.

By that time Cass had awakened hungry, surely a good sign. We all ate together in the attic, and the baby hardly cried. She was probably tired out. Getting born seemed a lot of work.

"Rest again, Miss Aurelia," I said. "I'll stay up late and read."

"Thank you. Wake me when you get sleepy. How are you, Cass? Bessie said your heart raced. How does it feel now?"

"Full of love." She turned to look at baby Hope. "I plan to mend real quick so we get ourselves up to Canada and free. This baby's name don't mean nothin' unless she get to the promised land and out of the reach of that old Mister Roberts."

"My brother will drive us, soon as you feel ready," I said.

"Amen," Cass said. "We going home soon. Can I write again in your book, Lucy?"

HOPE BORN FREE!

GLORY!

After Cass wrote, she fell back asleep. And so I sit here and admire the beautiful sight of Cass and her new daughter. Every time I look at the words Cass wrote, my eyes sting. Hope is so sweet, maybe someday I'll get brave enough to have a child after all.

SATURDAY, FEBRUARY 22, 1851
LATE AFTERNOON

I want to burn this journal. I hate the words I must write. I would burn down the whole house and the barns, with Miss Aurelia's blessing, if it would undo the past day and a half. But nothing can remove the shadow when the angel of death has passed by.

Cass is gone.

I can write no more.

SUNDAY, FEBRUARY 23, 1851
MORNING

Today is a black Sabbath. I can find no voice to sing hymns in Miss Aurelia's parlor. A blizzard has swept through my heart and frozen it.

Yet we have work to do and plans under way. Mama

told me I must write everything down, to honor Cass and to ease my pain. I will try, but I don't hold out much hope for success.

How could such a thing happen? Mrs. Smith says she's seen two other cases with the swelling legs and the racing heart. But I can't listen to her words, for my mind and heart rage. Why Cass? How could God let her die?

It happened in the small hours of Saturday morning. Miss Aurelia took over the watching about midnight, and by then I was yawning. I settled in under the quilt and fell right to sleep. It seemed like only minutes later when she shook my shoulder.

"Lucy. Lucy, there's trouble."

I sat right up and spoke the first thing that came into my head. "Catchers?"

"No—Cass. She shakes all over. Something's terribly wrong."

I jumped out of bed and ran to the attic. Cass and Hope lay on the pallet, just as I'd left them not two hours past. Miss Aurelia took my hand and led me closer. I could feel her fingers tremble.

"What happened? She looks fine."

"I almost missed it the first time. She didn't make noise, just began to shake. Her back arched up. The baby whimpered. Cass got quiet for a while. Then it happened again."

I felt Cass's head for fever, but she seemed cool. I couldn't see much in the darkness. "Is there a candle?"

"I'll find one," Miss Aurelia said.

I watched Cass as hard as I could, but the only thing that shook was me. I'd forgotten slippers, and my nightgown wasn't warm enough without bedcovers. I found a spare blanket and wrapped it around my shoulders.

Then I saw it. Cass began to shudder as if she too felt cold. She shook all over. Miss Aurelia came in with two lighted candles and a laundry basket. I could see Cass's eyes roll back until only the whites showed. Her mouth made strange, strangling sounds, and she seemed not able to breathe. Then the spasms passed, but only for a heartbeat. They started up again, worse than before.

Miss Aurelia hurried to the baby. She reached for Hope and tucked her into the laundry basket, out of harm's way.

I grabbed Cass's hands, which jumped at her sides. I tried to quiet her, but she was strong, and the shuddery, jerking spasms went on and on. I loosened my hold, afraid I'd bruise her arms. "Please, God," I prayed. "Take care of her for me. Make this go away."

Did He answer? At first I thought so, for it grew quiet, so quiet I could hear my heart thud in my chest and the sound of Miss Aurelia's breath, coming fast and harsh. But those were the only sounds in the room, those and a tiny squeak from Hope.

Cass lay still and absolutely silent. I placed my hand on her shoulder. No motion. Nothing. I felt for a heartbeat, for the movement of her chest as she breathed. Still nothing.

Miss Aurelia reached into her pocket and brought a mirror close to Cass's mouth and nose. "Get the candle so we can see."

I did as she said, but woodenly, liked a carved doll, for somehow I knew we would see nothing. In an instant Cass had gone—gone home, gone to freedom, leaving us behind.

I have eaten a meal, but whether it was corn bread or corncobs, I can't say, for I smell and taste nothing. I can barely speak. I feel as if a door has opened in my chest and icy air pours in.

My friend Cass is dead.

I still pray that I'll wake from this dreadful nightmare. But I don't. We'll bury Cass tonight.

When it first happened, Miss Aurelia and I held on to each other and stared at the bed, at Cass lying peaceful and still. We stood there a long time.

Then Miss Aurelia bent and picked up the laundry basket where the baby slept on, unaware. She passed the basket to me and stooped to straighten the covers around Cass.

"Come, Lucinda. We have much to do."

I followed her downstairs and watched her kneel to build up the fire. I still wore a blanket around my shoulders, and I huddled into it as I sat in a rocking chair with little Hope at my side and tried to get warm.

Miss Aurelia pressed her fingers to her temples and sat back on the raised hearth. "Where to begin, where to begin?" She looked up at me. "You know this will make everything more difficult," she said. "We must act, and quickly."

"I don't understand."

"We must bury her. But the ground is frozen. Above all else, we must safeguard the child."

I hadn't yet thought of the consequences of Cass's dying. My mind could hardly cope with the raw fact that she was gone. And yet if we were to keep the baby safe, Miss Aurelia was right. We had to act, and soon.

"I'd like to see Mama and Papa," I said.

"So you should. And we must inform the Strongs and Bessie Smith as well. How soon can you ride?"

In a daze I dressed and saddled the mare.

Snowy fields reflected the thin light of a waning moon as I rode, and I could see as if it were morning. Black trees, white snow, no color anywhere, only cold. I urged the horse on, for I felt chilled myself—not a chill of wind and snow, but a chill of death and dying. It numbed me to other feelings, and I simply rode.

I had never ridden alone at night before. Some other night, on some different errand, I might have found it exhilarating. But I could barely contain my sorrow—Cass, dead—so I boxed the sadness tightly in my chest and froze it solid like pond ice so that it wouldn't overpower me. Dear God, I was so tired and cold.

Emma, Cass, and the children had traveled in the coldest hours of the night. How frightening for a person used to warm southern nights to be suddenly exposed to lake storms and blizzards. I studied the sky. I found the Big Dipper and the North Star, imagined them as my only map.

I neared the curve that marked the last mile before our farm. Hoofbeats. I pulled the mare up and listened. Two horses at least.

I dismounted and led the mare to a hedgerow, where weedy trees and brush marked the edge of a field. I hid her in the shadows and stood where I could watch the road but remain unseen.

The hoofbeats grew louder, and creaking wood told me that a wagon traveled as well. I held the mare's mouth to keep her quiet. Only two sorts of people went out driving wagons in the middle of the night: rescuers and catchers. Lord help me, but if that Clayton Roberts rode by me tonight, I wouldn't be able to restrain myself. I'd do him damage for certain.

I held my breath and watched the curve in the road. The minutes crawled. At last the wagon rounded the curve in half shadow. As it drew closer I saw a single driver wearing an old-fashioned wide-brimmed hat. I stared as the wagon came close.

Thanks be to God.

I stepped from the shadows onto the edge of the road. "Jeremiah?" I said. "Jeremiah Strong?"

When Jeremiah's arms went around me, the ice jam inside broke up. My sorrow burst loose and I shook with all the sobs I'd been holding back.

"She's . . . she's gone."

"The baby?"

"Cass. Oh, Jeremiah!"

"No!"

"Jeremiah, she was my friend. Only nineteen. Just three years older than I am."

He stood there with me at the side of the road and held me.

I raged and cried out my grief. When I had exhausted

the tears he boosted me up to the seat, rounded up the mare, and hitched her to the back of his wagon.

"I'm taking thee home," he said.

"But—you travel at night. Wayfarers?"

"Yes. Two. In thy parents' care. But we must get thee home."

"It's not safe, Jeremiah. I can ride alone. I'll be all right."

"No." He drove with one hand and kept the other arm around me, steadying me.

When we reached our house Papa came out. "Lucinda! What brings you here in the middle of the night?"

"Bad news," I said. I ran to him, and the well of tears I'd thought empty spilled over again on his shoulder.

I told Papa about Cass. "We—We'll gather at Miss Aurelia's," I stammered. "Tomorrow afternoon."

"My family will be there," Jeremiah said.

"Thank you for bringing me home. I was so tired." In truth, I might not have made that last long mile without Jeremiah's warm, strong arm tight around me.

"Sleep now. Thy family will give thee comfort." He took my hand. "I admire thy strength, Lucinda. Not many girls would ride out alone at night. Until tomorrow."

Papa led me into the house. Mama was awake, and as she took me in her arms I cried again. She patted my back and comforted me as if I were a child like Miranda. I felt her love and kindness warm my icy soul, and I drifted into a dreamless sleep.

I shall need Mama's arms around me again tonight as I stand by the grave in the Quaker cemetery and bid farewell to Cass. How can God be so cruel?

———

I've never attended a sadder funeral. Clouds drifted across the night sky, and only a dim sliver of moon showed. We'd bundled ourselves in dark clothes and hats and stood in the graveyard.

In the burying ground behind their meeting house, the Quakers prepare a few graves each fall for any who die when the ground is hard. Jeremiah had selected a grave far back from the road, where a thick oak shielded us. Still, we didn't dare stay long or make noise.

We stood in a circle, Papa with his arm around Will, then Mama and me. I held the baby. Miss Aurelia, on my other side, had agreed that we should bring Hope. When she was grown, she'd be glad. The Smiths stood with Miss Aurelia, and Jeremiah's family finished the circle.

We whispered prayers as the men lowered the coffin into the grave. Without intending it, I began the words of the familiar psalm, "The Lord is my shepherd . . ." The others joined in, and we said the words slowly, softly, to bless Cass on her way. Tears wet my cheeks, and I brushed them aside.

We stood quiet awhile, as the Quakers do. Then Mrs. Smith began to sing, her voice soft and mournful. "Steal away, steal away, steal away to Jesus! Steal away, steal away home, I ain't got long to stay here."

I felt my cheeks grow wet again, but I lifted my voice and joined in. Emma had taught me that song. Cass would like it as her benediction.

Dear Cass. She'd lived a hard life, a woman's life, yet

we'd laughed together as girls. I hadn't known her long, but we'd become friends. For her to die now, on the very edge of freedom . . . it felt so wrong.

For comfort, I held tight to Hope. Hope, so well named. Cass had not survived, but Hope would go on. Hope would endure. I would see to it. That thought eased my heart as the men lifted their first shovelfuls of dirt to fill in the grave. I would carry Hope to freedom. Nothing would stand in my way.

And so I sit here and mourn my friend. I try to warm myself, but without success, for a chill is always with me. Nineteen is much too young to die.

MONDAY, FEBRUARY 24, 1851

At last some of the ice leaves my heart. Anger burns hot and fine and melts it away. I long to pour my rage out in letters—to President Fillmore for signing that dreadful law, to Clayton Roberts for his evil lechery, to his wife for her killing jealousy. But anger begets anger, and such letters would only stir up trouble. I need a cool head, for I have more to do. I'll write to Jeremiah, for courage.

24 *February*

Dear Jeremiah,

Guard this page carefully, for my heart aches and I haven't the energy or cleverness to write with hidden meanings today.

I'm not at home, but with Miss Aurelia, for I feel a great warmth for Hope, my only connection to Cass. She seems to return my affection. When I hold her, she stops crying. Just now she sleeps, all sweet and rosy in the laundry basket as I write.

My Friend, I'm not sure I would have reached home that awful night without your help. My heart was so heavy, I might just have drifted into a snowbank, frozen, and joined Cass on her heavenward journey. But God sent you for me, and you carried me home to my family. I thank you for all your kindness.

Now I ask your assistance again. I must carry the child to Canada. Mrs. Smith has offered to find a nearby colored family to raise her, but I cannot allow that. Emma must be told of her sister's death and must have the child. And since Hope seems most content with me, I shall take her myself. Mama and Papa tried to discourage me. But as neither of them could devise a better scheme, they have reluctantly agreed.

I will ride north with my brother and pose as a young wife with a new baby, rejoining my husband in Cleveland. Might you and your sister speak with Will and devise a travel plan? For you know the routes and all the best places to stay. If I can keep Hope's dark curls covered, I believe she will pass as white, for her skin is mostly rosy.

Please help me with this journey, dear Jeremiah, for some part of me won't begin to heal until I have completed this mission.

I am your most grateful and heartsore friend,
Lucinda

TUESDAY, FEBRUARY 25, 1851

Is there anything like a baby? Hope smells sweeter than a field of spring flowers. She keeps my spirits from plunging into despair when she snuggles into my shoulder and mews like a kitten. Yet sadness returns again and again.

Will came today. He will carry my letter to Jeremiah and bring news and a reply as soon as he can. Now that I have made up my mind to travel, I find waiting a wretched waste of time.

Wednesday, February 26, 1851

Anger got hold of me again today and I snapped at Miss Aurelia. When I apologized, she patted my shoulder and passed me a sheet of paper.

"I'll send it out once you have returned and the child is safe," she said.

24 February

To William Lloyd Garrison, for publication in
The Liberator—

A Voice from the Wilderness

The powers of darkness have claimed another victory and liberty has suffered another loss. In the free Northern state of Ohio a woman has died, leaving an orphaned babe behind. And for what reason? Slavery.

Whips and chains are not enough, no! Now the slave owners must deprive people of life itself. This woman, barely more than a girl, was forced to run away to protect herself and her expected child from an evil master who misused her. He chased after, intoxicated with lust and power.

Birthing the child he forced upon her, the young woman died. Her child, born in freedom, can yet be carried back to slavery. Is there justice in this land? I hear the Almighty's voice, admonishing us to make straight the highway of our God. And yet we travel a twisted path instead of His golden road. How long must we go on? How long must we allow this dark shadow of human bondage to defile our land?

Before she died, the woman named her child Hope. We must fulfill her dying wish and provide hope for all who are in chains. As men and women of conscience, we must prevail to lift the evil shadow and return our nation to the sunlight of God's love and word. For hope must endure. We are nothing if we cannot protect an innocent child, a gift of God.

Miss Aurelia's words stir my heart to action. It feels good to know that I am not the only one who fumes and rages.

THURSDAY, FEBRUARY 27, 1851

Hope is a week old today. I wish I felt like celebrating.

FRIDAY, FEBRUARY 28, 1851

Will has returned with a plan and supplies for our journey. He also recited a list of cautions as long as my arm, from Mama and Papa. Mama offered to make the trip herself in my place, but Papa convinced her that my youth and innocence will make our story seem more true.

Mama sent me Grandmother's gold ring to wear in imitation of a married woman. I hope we aren't stopped and that we don't need to playact, but I will ride easier with my parents' blessings and that worn golden circle on my finger. I doubt Mama and Papa would even consider letting me make this trip if it weren't for my brother Will and his well-traveled wagon, so I am many times blessed.

We leave for Ravenna at dawn tomorrow. I like it that our journey will begin on the first day of March. February has brought gray skies and sadness. Good riddance!

MARCH

A bitter and chill darkness sits upon my heart this day, for all our brave, bright beginnings. William and I did as planned. Our story was good enough, or so we thought. I was a young wife and had gone home to Mama to bear my child. My brother carried me north, back to my pretend husband.

We traveled well all day, making quick work of the miles between Atwater and Ravenna. Hope slept the journey away, for I'd dosed her with paregoric Mama sent. We reached Ravenna before dark. Will pulled up in front of a largish inn and unloaded my trunk and our food on the porch.

"You get us signed in and feed that baby. I'll tend the horses," he said. "Somebody from the inn will help with the carrying."

He pulled away. I entered the inn and sniffed the rich smell of beef roasting. My mouth watered. I turned to find the innkeeper when something blocked my path.

"Is that you, Lucinda Spencer? What the dickens are you doing here? And what do you have in your arms?"

My breath caught. I turned and looked straight into the face of that old slippery snake of a deputy, Levi Bowen. And worse, behind him stood the man whose child I carried: Clayton Roberts.

Levi Bowen grabbed my arm. "This looks mighty suspicious, missy. You ain't going nowhere till we get some answers."

Clayton Roberts eased Levi aside as though he were no more substantial than a lace window curtain. "We do require answers," he said, smiling at me. "But there's no need to be uncivilized."

My skin crawled. How dare he talk about being civilized? As the two men led me to a table I realized the depth of my difficulty. We'd designed a story for strangers, not for someone who knew us. I'd have to think of something to tell them, and quickly.

Will walked in. I nodded and blinked in warning. He caught my meaning and backed out of sight.

My mind sped through my choices as I sat, hugging Hope for dear life. But everything narrowed to one question. What must I do to prevent them from taking the baby back to slavery?

The innkeeper greeted us and promised coffee.

"Lucinda," Levi Bowen began, "explain about the child."

Papa always says to look at people directly, so I did. I took a deep breath. "She's my child. Her name is Hope."

"I'll see the babe," Clayton Roberts said. "If you don't mind."

Of course I minded, but what could I do? I laid Hope on the tabletop and loosened her blankets. Once my hands were free, I slipped the ring from my finger and into my skirt pocket, for our intended story would only cause more suspicion now.

Roberts pulled off Hope's cap and exposed a soft tangle of dark curls. "She looks like a colored child," he said. "I have experience with such people, you understand. How could a young lady such as yourself come to have a colored child?"

How indeed? "She is half colored and half white," I replied with a shaking voice.

"Damnation," Levi Bowen shouted. "You expect us to believe this hogwash? You're a sheltered young girl, Lucinda, from a good Christian family. You ain't about to fornicate with no black man. I say she's a slave child." He glared at me. "I'll lock you up, girl, if you're harboring a runaway."

"It looks rather likely," Clayton Roberts said.

My heart galloped faster than a team of horses. I looked into Hope's tiny face for inspiration but found none. All I could do was make a story up as I went along.

"I was trying to get out of town. Up to Cleveland, where nobody knows me. It's a big town. I could raise the child in secret."

Sounded credible to me, and it explained why I traveled this road with my trunk.

"Now, Miss Spencer," Clayton Roberts began, as if I were six, "a slave of mine escaped. She was expecting a child, and that child would have arrived by now. I have a strong notion that this child is my property." He looked into the baby's face and studied it carefully. "I wonder what you did with her mother."

I took a deep breath to keep from spitting in his face.

"Do I look like the sort of person who would do something with someone's mother? I'm not a baby-stealer. Hope is my own child. I stayed with Widow Mercer so no one would see my condition. You saw me there. I gave birth to the child at her house. Please, I've kept my secret so far—have pity on me and spread the story no further."

My mind skidded back to the days he'd come to Miss Aurelia's. I'd worn a long, heavy woolen dress and a big apron both times. Enough clothing to hide a bulging belly? I surely hoped so.

I lowered my head, as if ashamed. "Please, sirs. I've made mistakes, but I don't mean to hurt anybody. I just want to go away where nobody knows me. Where this child and I won't be scorned."

Levi Bowen snorted. "Ain't no place a child like that

won't make trouble. Even supposing you're telling the truth."

Clayton Roberts shook his head. "I have grave doubts about your story," he said, "but we'll offer you a chance to prove it. Bowen, who is the preacher at that Presbyterian church?"

"The Atwater church? The Reverend Cummings," Bowen said. "He's a good man. Virginian."

"Married?" Roberts asked. I wondered what he was getting at.

"Yep. Mrs. Cummings is a Virginia gal. Loyal, upstanding folks."

"Fine. I'll send for the Reverend's wife, then. And the local doctor," Roberts said.

He turned and smiled at me, looking very sure of himself. "The doctor will examine you in the presence of a good and virtuous woman who knows you well. They will certify whether you are or are not the child's mother. If you are, then you may do as you please, travel to Cleveland or wherever. But if you are not, Mr. Bowen will write out a warrant for your arrest. Until then you'll be held here under guard. Do we understand each other?"

I nodded. I understood all too well. I had no choice. If I argued or protested my innocence, they'd condemn me as guilty. My future and the future of this tiny child lay in the hands of some strange doctor and Mrs. Cummings. I hugged the baby close to keep from crying out loud.

I couldn't think of a worse fate.

Levi Bowen arranged for me to be put in a room on the second floor. He and the innkeeper hauled up my trunk and boxes and nosed into them before they left me alone.

Hope whimpered, and I laid her on the bed to unwrap her from the blankets. I felt like bawling, too, for at least a week, but I had to feed the baby first. I took off my own heavy clothes and dug into a basket for her jug of milk. I poured some into a smaller jar and set it beside the fire to warm. At least I had the comfort of a fire.

As I reached into the basket for the rubber teat to stretch over the mouth of the jar, I felt paper. Will had somehow managed to sneak in a note.

Lucy, you're in real deep trouble. What should I do? Run for Papa and Jeremiah Strong, or bust you out of here myself? There's only the two of them right now. We could do it. I heard them say you'd have to stay here for a day or two. But they'll get more men tomorrow, so we'd best hurry. Hang the baby's cap in the window so I know which room to watch. Be careful. William.

Thank God for William. But what could we do? I hung Hope's cap in the window, as he'd asked, and thought about it as I changed her and fed her from the jar of milk.

If Will and I somehow managed to escape, we wouldn't get far. They'd watch the roads. Tomorrow Clayton Roberts would set up more men to guard me. And tomorrow Mrs. Cummings would come with some strange doctor. So I didn't have much time. I had to leave right away. I checked the window. The light was pale, late afternoon. Whatever we did, it would be safer by night. I tried to think of plans for escape, but instead panic filled my mind.

A thousand-dollar fine. We'd lose the farm. But we'd helped ten people—a ten-thousand-dollar fine! Impossible. Papa, Mama, Miss Aurelia, Mrs. Smith, the Strongs—they'd all be ruined. I'd go to jail. Worst of all, Hope would have to go back to Carolina and live as a slave. I held her tight as she sucked milk from the jar. I either had to escape or convince people that I really was Hope's mother.

And if I did that? Then what? Last year a hired girl south of town had a baby without a husband. People acted real ugly, and her baby was white. The baby I claimed was half colored. People would call me a sinner and worse. They'd want to know who the father was, and they'd go after him with tar and feathers or else a hanging rope. They'd come after me. They'd blame Mama and Papa for my sins, punish my brothers and sister.

Fools! Their eyes would pop if I told who the real father was. That vile Clayton Roberts. His face appeared before my eyes, handsome and sure of himself and so slick. It made me mad, mad enough to stop feeling sorry for myself. I would escape from that man's reach! I would save this baby!

And I realized, suddenly, that I had nearly everything I needed to get away. I might just pull it off.

Without stopping to burp Hope, I laid her on the bed and scribbled a note to my brother. I stood beside the window and watched. Nothing moved. I opened the window. It creaked slightly. Below me the shadows stirred.

"Will?" I whispered.

"Lucy. Quick."

I dropped the note and stepped away from the window. I quickly scribbled another note for Mama and Papa.

1 *March*

Dear Mama and Papa,

You were so right to worry about my journey. We are caught! Clayton Roberts was staying at the inn in Ravenna. I bumped into him this afternoon as we arrived and he discovered the child. Oh, Papa! Does nothing ever go according to plan? Is God truly on our side in this, or does He forget us?

My only hope lies in William, who was tending to the horses when I was discovered. Will ducked into the barn and hid. Now we have a plan of sorts. It's risky but, I think, the only way. Once Will has carried me where I need to go, he will return to warn all of you. Do as he asks, please. Go along with my story.

Someone must take responsibility for what has happened. I am that someone. Will, Tom, and Miranda are young. They still need you. They need our home. I'm grown and can manage a life on my own, at least for a while. I was nearing the time when I'd begin my life as a woman, anyway. But Mama, in all the times we talked about it, I never suspected that I'd have to leave you all behind.

I can't write any more, for I will lose my courage, whatever is left of it. Keep us ever in your prayers.

Love,
Lucinda

Now all I can do is wait for nightfall and pray for deliverance. Someone knocks at the door. I must hide this deep in my trunk and see who it is.

SATURDAY, MARCH 1, 1851
LATER

The sun is at the horizon and I am ready at last, but the waiting still jangles my nerves. How long now? An hour, perhaps? Can I endure it? I must, for I have endured worse this day.

Bah on both my visitors! They each made me quite sick.

Clayton Roberts knocked at my door first. He didn't even wait for me to invite him in, just strode across the room as though he owned it. "Miss Spencer. May I call you Lucinda?"

I turned and glared at him.

He stood quite close to me, and I could smell spirits on his breath. "My dear. This is quite a tangle for a young girl such as yourself. Perhaps we can arrive at some compromise." He took my chin in his hand and turned my face toward his.

"You are quite lovely, you know. And if you have given yourself to a colored man, or even if you have thought of doing such a thing, perhaps a man such as myself won't displease you. I've been told I'm not hard to look at." His blue eyes glittered.

I wanted to pull away, but I didn't dare. He could yank Hope from the bed and take her south in a blink. "Please, sir . . ."

"If you were to tell me the whereabouts of my property, Lucinda dear,"—he brushed my cheek with his fingers—"and if you were to assist me in finding all that I own, I might be inclined to forgo punishment, drop all complaints. If you were to ask me sweetly . . . and offer me some other reward for my forgiveness."

What was he asking? That I lead him to Abraham and Emma? And then what? Lie with him? Never!

My mind scrambled for an answer, then hit on words I'd heard from Mrs. Smith at the birthing. I stepped away. "Please, sir. I've just borne a child. My condition is tender. . . ."

"Dinner for you, miss."

Bless her, whoever she was. A woman with a tray. She was stout and not very tall and she scowled at me. "They said we was to feed you." She glared past me at the baby, sleeping sweet as a lamb on the bed, and then at Clayton Roberts.

"We'll speak again, Lucinda," he said. "I'll leave you to your meal."

He left, and I caught my breath.

"If I had my way, I'd make it bread and water for a shameless hussy like you." The woman passed me the tray, then stomped down the hall.

I stood at the door and swallowed, amazed by the woman's anger. She didn't even know me, yet she hated me. How much worse would it be in my own village, where people knew me and would sharpen their teeth on the gossip? I closed my eyes and imagined Jonathan Clark's mother, her nose in the air, sniffing as though I smelled of spoiled meat.

Levi Bowen stepped up to guard my door. He pointed to the tray I clutched. "You can thank Mr. Roberts for that tasty dinner. The bread pudding is especially fine. She added a good measure of rum. You won't eat nearly so well in the magistrate's jail."

His words made me want to choke, but I held back my temper and closed the door on his nasty grin. He liked the bread pudding, did he? And it had rum in it. That helped.

I had no appetite, but I made myself eat the roast beef and boiled potatoes. The woman had put coffee as well as milk on my tray, and I blessed her for that, in spite of her rudeness. The coffee would keep me awake. I needed my mind alert if I was to succeed.

I watched at the window for a time, waiting for the sky to darken and wishing for home. But wishing won't undo this day's wickedness, so instead I imagine a vision of home, to ease my heart: Miranda is settling down to sleep. I've just finished reading her a story. Mama is knitting and rocking. Papa reads the weekly paper. Will mends harness while Tom whittles—perhaps a boat, a whistle, or a small animal for Miranda. If only my vision could come true.

I hold Grandmother's ring tight in my hand and my eyes fill. No matter what happens, I won't be able to go home again. Not for a long time. I've set loose a deep river of lies and secrets, and I've burned all my boats. What will happen beyond this moment, beyond this night and the task I have set for myself?

If I get myself and this sweet bundle named Hope out of Ravenna and into Canada, what will I do with my life then? I can't return home and bring shame and hatred to my family. Where will I go instead?

I haven't the slightest notion.

SUNDAY, MARCH 2, 1851

It is morning and I am in hiding. Somewhere people celebrate the Sabbath and sing hymns of praise. I simply whisper a prayer of thanks. God has not forgotten us after all, in spite of the dreadful night we passed.

When it finally grew dark enough I woke the baby and let her work up to a good holler. I fed her a jar of milk with a half spoon of paregoric mixed in. That would buy a few hours of silence. I patted her and she drifted back to sleep. "Sorry I have to give you that old medicine," I said. "But it's only for a few days. Then you can yell and holler all you want."

When she was sound asleep again, I opened my door. Sure enough, Levi Bowen sat on a chair right outside. I set my dinner tray on the floor next to him.

"Change your mind yet? Ready to tell the truth?" he asked.

I glared at him. "You wouldn't know truth if it walked up and shook hands with you," I said. "Tell Mr. Roberts thank you for the dinner. I ate some, but I wasn't much hungry."

"Didn't eat the bread pudding? You missed a treat."

"Help yourself. That woman downstairs will eat it if you don't."

"Don't mind if I do. She's stout enough already." He picked up my dish and grinned.

"There's milk too, if you'd like."

He nodded, and I poured it for him as though I were helping Mama entertain the church ladies. I smiled, a real smile, because the milk, added to the rum, would disguise the taste of the paregoric I'd mixed into the bread pudding. I'd used half the bottle and prayed it was enough.

I returned to my room and made the rest of my preparations. I hoped I'd sound as though I was getting ready for bed. I got out my nightgown and stuffed it full of petticoats and shirtwaists from my trunk, until I thought it looked about my size. Then I arranged it carefully under the covers, with a skirt rolled up in a baby blanket close by. I added a small cap to the baby-sized lump and stuffed it with handkerchiefs.

I pulled on a pair of Will's trousers, his extra pair of boots, and a heavy knitted vest of mine. I stuffed the trousers and vest with as many of Hope's clothes as I could fit, then added Will's old woolen jacket. I tucked all of the money Papa had sent for our journey, the ring, and a pair of mittens into the pockets. I carefully braided my hair and pinned it up, hiding as much as I could under a knitted cap. I examined myself in the looking glass on the chest of drawers. If one didn't look too closely, I could pass for a boy . . . a plump boy, for all the baby's things filled up my clothing.

I added another layer of warmth to the baby and wrapped her securely in two blankets. I kissed her soft little cheek. "This has to work, Hope. It just has to."

She nuzzled my neck in her sleep, and I was tempted for a moment to live the lie I'd told Clayton Roberts: to go to Cleveland, disappear in a crowded neighborhood, and raise her myself. But no. I had Emma to think about, and Cass.

My preparations took nearly half an hour. Was that enough? I listened at the door. Nothing. I'd hoped Levi Bowen would snore, so that I'd know if I'd put him to sleep, but he didn't. I opened the door a crack. Still no sounds. If he was awake, I'd say I needed warm water to wash the baby.

Luck was on my side at last. Levi Bowen sagged back in his chair, his head tipped to one side, breathing slow, even breaths. I eased myself and Hope out the door and pulled it shut. I slipped past him like a cat.

At the end of the hall there were two sets of stairs— the main staircase, a fancy one, and a back stair, which probably led to the kitchen. I took that one, praying none of the steps would creak.

As I descended I heard voices to my left. The brick wall on the right felt cold. Was that the way outdoors? I moved down one careful step at a time. The voices got louder, still from the left. Either they would discover me or their noise would hide me. I clutched Hope closer to my chest and stepped down onto the landing.

I felt the two doors at the bottom. The right was cold. I turned the latch and pushed slightly. It creaked. I held my breath. Nobody came. I pushed again and peered out. Fresh, cold air. Stars. So far I had guessed right. I eased outside and looked around to get my bearings.

I stood at the back of the inn. I listened for the sound of horses. Will was to wait for me at the stable. I couldn't hear horses, but as I sniffed, I caught the scent of manure and followed it, slipping from shadow to shadow like a thief.

At last I reached the stable. No lights showed. Had Will been successful with his part of the plan? As I reached to open the door a shape came out of the darkness.

"Lucy?"

"Will. Thank God."

He hugged me, and I could feel his bony shoulders tremble.

"Did you do it?" I asked. I reached into my jacket. "Here, tie these blankets around me in a sling for the baby."

He fumbled with the knots. "I did like you said. Let's get moving. We can talk as we go."

I nodded and fell into step beside Will. I shifted Hope until she rode easy. Will led us across a pasture, muddy with spring thaw.

"I got a message to the Quaker doctor. He expects you tonight. If anything goes wrong, he'll examine you tomorrow or the next day. He'll say you are the baby's mother, if you still want that."

"I hope I don't need to, but yes, that's the plan."

Will shook his head. "I wish you wouldn't, Lucy. People ain't going to forget this. You'll never be able to live a regular life again, not in our town."

"I know. But what choice do I have?"

He shook his head. "Watch out here. There's a house close. Sneak behind the trees." He took my hand and I clambered after, across rough roots and branches. I hugged Hope tight with my other arm, glad she was securely tied.

"Will, tell me about the wagon."

"I did what you asked. I laid a false trail nearly to Hudson. Wagon's hidden now, in a barn. The farmer helps with the Railroad. He loaned me a saddle horse. He'll care for my team."

"Good. And the Quaker doctor? He's helped us before, hasn't he? With other rescues."

Will nodded. "His house is a mile and a half by the road. But we're going roundabout, away from town. He's making plans. I left the horse there so I could go home and warn everybody. But Lucy . . . I ain't going home. I'm going with you. If anything happens and I'm not there . . ." Will's voice cracked.

My eyes filled. "Please, Will. I've thought about this all evening. You must go. You must warn Mama and Papa, Miss Aurelia, and Jeremiah. Those men will hunt for me starting tomorrow. It's bad enough I got caught. We can't have more trouble."

"I still think—"

"Will, do this for me. I'll travel safer on my own, with just Hope. We'll be easier to hide."

"I'll do it, but I don't like it," he grumbled.

After an hour of difficult walking we crossed a muddy lane and Will pointed toward a cluster of buildings. "Doc Harding lives there. So far we've had luck tonight. If it keeps up, you'll have a whale of an adventure. I wish I could go, too."

An adventure. I used to think like that. But things have changed. I've changed.

"No, Will. This isn't about adventure," I said, putting both arms around the baby. "This is about saving lives. I'm scared, really scared."

He threw an arm around me and we walked up the path. Will knocked at the door, two short raps. He waited, knocked twice more.

"Who's there?" asked a man's voice from within.

"A Friend with a friend," Will said.

How many times have I heard just those words when I stand on the other side of the door? Now I'm the friend on the outside. How odd. How very, very odd.

MONDAY, MARCH 3, 1851

And so I travel the Railroad.

Dr. Harding said he thought the Cleveland docks would be watched, so he routed us north and east toward Ashtabula and a place they call "Mother Hubbard's cupboard." Last night Hope and I lay in a coffin for hours as an undertaker's wagon bounced along the long road between Ravenna and Chardon.

As I lay there, jostling against the hard, splintery wooden boards, I clasped Hope to my breast and thought about death and dying. About the baby Mama lost last spring. About the mama this baby lost just last week.

Now I'll lose more. I can't return home. My heart tears when I count up the people I love. Mama and Papa, Will, Tom, and Miranda—I bring their faces to my mind, gathering them as if they were perishable as summer raspberries. I store them in my memory for the days and weeks to come. Rebecca, Miss Aurelia, Jeremiah Strong.

Jonathan Clark. Even the Cummings family, people I don't particularly like, grow dear to me at the thought of parting.

Riding in a coffin seems so proper somehow. I mourn all the people I love and cannot return to. More, I mourn my old self. I shall write an obituary—

There once was a girl, a young woman almost, Lucinda Spencer by name. She loved adventures, that girl did, and pranks and mischief. She thought herself a romantic heroine, admired by two young men. She was pleased with herself for having to decide between them. But admiration wasn't enough; she wanted to stretch her wings and fly out into the world. Now she is a wild goose who wings her way to Canada with no notion of the flyway home.

TUESDAY, MARCH 4, 1851

Chardon at last. It took two nights of hard travel, and my back is so sore that even the rough straw in this hayloft feels good.

Chardon. The name reminds me of something. From my studies. If I leave out the *d* . . . Charon. Is that it? The mythical boatman who ferries dead souls across the river Styx. How very appropriate, for we still ride in a narrow coffin and will soon be carried across the water, never to return home. Oh, Mama! Papa! I miss you so much!

It didn't have to be this way—I didn't have to get caught. Why didn't I travel the Railroad from the start? Perhaps our grief numbed our minds and blurred our caution? Perhaps my white skin gave me the illusion of protection? But there is no protection.

No one is safe from slavery. It destroys people, as it did Cass. It breaks apart families, as it did Emma's . . . and now mine. I'm learning terrible lessons, I who like playing teacher.

Through Concord and on to Fairport last night. These names ring with bitter irony. Concord—agreement, peacefulness. I carry no such feelings in my heart. And if the port I rest in this day is fair, I don't know it, for I hide in a dark, dank cellar. I embarked upon this wretched journey to save Hope, yet it is the child who saves me. For when despair washes over me and my tears flow, she curls closer and warms my frozen spirit. Dear Cass, if only you could have known your daughter. She is sweet and so beautiful, even under these dreadful circumstances.

I am getting better at sleeping in the coffin. I woke only once during the night's trip from Fairport to Ellensbury, and finally to Ashtabula. We hide this day in Mother Hubbard's cupboard. I would laugh at the name if I could remember how to laugh. A ship's captain named Hubbard lives in this house, quite near to the lake. He has dug out a passage from the hidden room where we rest to the shore. When tomorrow night comes we will creep out and wait for a boat to Canada. And then what? Exile?

As I sit here in the gloom, I remember Miss Aurelia's clean, spacious attic. I think about playing school up there with Cass. I could do that, at least. Perhaps I could stay awhile in Canada and teach people to read and cipher. It would fill up my days.

I could teach not just one family but many, former slaves who want to learn. At the thought of teaching, I feel something that resembles a smile steal across my face. For the first time since I saw the awful face of Clayton Roberts in Ravenna, life flows in my veins, as if someday I might be whole again.

Miss Aurelia's face comes to mind. She has a life of her own, a good life. She thinks women are strong. That they can overcome difficulties, make choices. That there is more to life than marrying this boy or that one.

I can make choices.

Shall I spend the rest of my life alone? No. I'll write letters. People who care about me will write back, and visit. Windsor, Canada, isn't the end of the earth. I could train to be a real teacher, attend college someday. Mama and Papa will help with that if I ask.

And Jeremiah. I can choose Jeremiah Strong if I wish. I know that when this is all over, he will find me. Or else I will find him.

FRIDAY, MARCH 7, 1851
LATE

Lake Erie at last . . .

Tonight I stood at the rail of a lake steamer and watched the crew pull up the gangplank and unhitch ropes from the mooring poles. I felt the water surge under the boat, and my heart hummed.

As the engines roared to life I held Hope toward the shoreline. "See? We're on our way. Say goodbye to your old life, baby."

Cold air gusted toward us, and Hope wailed. I tucked her back inside the warmth of my coat and watched the lights on the horizon move, glimmer, and fade away. The ribbon of water between us and the shore widened as our steamer plowed through dark waters.

Hope and I were on our way. I slipped Grandmother's thin gold band onto my finger, for luck and for remembrance.

I thought about the path that had led to this voyage and wondered. If I had it to do over, would I make the same choices? Work the Railroad? Save this baby? Leave home forever? If I got pushed to the edge, I might. But I might not. I'm not as brave as I'd always thought I was. Nor as wise.

And yet I've helped save lives. Many lives in the past four years. Ten very special lives in this case. That eases the hurt some.

As I looked down at the dark water, churned up by powerful engines, I thought of my life—it spun and whirled like the water. Would it ever grow calm again?

Do I want calm? Or do I instead want new shape to my life, new meaning? I like the sound of that. I was considering my future in a small town with only the familiar to choose from. Suddenly I have the world.

I looked into Hope's eyes and saw life there. Freedom.

"Not a bad place to start, sweet baby," I said. "With luck, we'll find the courage to grow into strong women—

like your mama and mine. And the spirit to become original ones—like Miss Aurelia."

I smiled, took a deep breath of the misty lake air, and
hugged Hope to my breast.

A girl could do worse.

KATHERINE AYRES has been a lover of children's books since childhood. Born in Columbus, Ohio, she began inventing stories before she could write them. Her love of literature continued through her first career as a teacher and elementary-school principal. She currently writes fiction for adults and for children.

Katherine Ayres lives in Pittsburgh, where she skis, golfs, gardens, quilts, teaches at Chatham College, and rebuilds old houses between writing sessions. She has written a play titled *Park Amusements,* which will be produced in New York City. Katherine Ayres's first novel, *Family Tree,* is on several state reading lists.